Praise for the New England Romances of Virginia Young

"Trust Virginia Young to take you on a mini-vacation with her warm, engaging stories. The characters become dear friends as you follow their journeys and longings in lovely settings in New England."
~Kathy Handley, author of Birds of Paradise and a *world of love and envy: short stories, flash fiction, and poetry* and Massachusetts Resident

"A fabulous romantic read...rich characters and sense of (local) place...I feel as though Virginia is sitting with me over a cup of coffee and telling me this great story."
~Mary Casey, librarian and Massachusetts Resident

"Warm cider for the soul!"
~Michael Martioski, DJ and New Hampshire Resident

"Virginia's books are one of my favorite guilty pleasures."
~PJ Schott, writer and Massachusetts Resident

"The plot, characters and descriptions in Out of the Blue make for a wonderful book to curl up with and read..."
~Marie McBride, writer and Massachusetts Resident

Sleepless Tides

Sleepless Tides

a romance
set in Maine

Virginia Young

Riverhaven Books

www.RiverhavenBooks.com

Sleepless Tides is a work of fiction. While some of the settings in Maine are actual, any similarity regarding names, characters, or incidents is entirely coincidental.

Published in the United States by Riverhaven Books,
www.RiverhavenBooks.com

ISBN: 978-1-937588-24-3

Printed in the United States of America
by Country Press, Lakeville, Massachusetts

Designed and Edited by Stephanie Lynn Blackman
Whitman, MA

In Memory Of
Skippy, Scooter, Dragon, Bubbles, and Oscar

Special thanks to
Sesa and Ed
for their editing skills
and
encouragement

Chapter One

When she'd last seen Meg, Lindsay had been thirteen and attending the traumatic funeral for her parents – now, she was twenty-eight.

"Cliff Point is secluded, yet lively," Meg had written in her last letter. There were civilian law department positions available at the nearby Navy facility, positions for which Lindsay was more than qualified. People of all ages worked at the base and Lindsay decided it could be a good beginning. Even though she wasn't financially dependant on getting work right away, she knew that the position at the Navy base would serve to involve her - she needed that commitment to life again. The trust her parents left remained untouched, and she still had the account which she had shared with Peter.

The drive from Boston to Maine seemed long. As dusk drew near, Lindsay arrived at a misty Cliff Point - the smell of salt air penetrated the closed windows of her car and the cry of the gulls was muffled by the engine as she hesitated at a stop sign.

Meg had described her home as being on a hill, large, white, and on the main street. Lindsay found it easily, for it stood slightly above and yet among other older homes facing the street and the open sea.

Before she took the turn toward Meg's lengthy driveway, she looked in her rearview mirror, to the left and to the right before proceeding. As she began to pull away from the stop sign, a car pulled up beside her, passing her with an impatient glare from the driver's accusing eyes.

"Thanks for the welcome to Cliff Point," she said aloud, hoping that this person was not going to be an example of the town's hospitality. She noted that he drove a sporty yet practical looking dark blue vehicle, not a model she was accustomed to seeing.

Lindsay moved the fifty or so yards toward Meg's circular driveway and parked within a few feet of the front door. She glanced into her rearview mirror and thought that her shoulder length dark hair could use a good brushing. Instead, she pushed and pulled at it carelessly and then thought about her entire disheveled appearance after traveling in the car for several hours. The pale blue denim jeans were okay, and the white jersey would pass, but she thought that her light weight denim jacket was in need of a good pressing. As she sat reviewing herself critically, Meg appeared at the driver's side window and tapped on the glass.

Lindsay smiled, turned the ignition off, then opened the car door and stepped out, hugging her diminutive friend.

"Lindsay Jane Heddon, look at you. You're so beautiful. Oh, Honey, I'm so glad you're here."

"I'm a mess I think," Lindsay said, smoothing her jeans. "I feel crumpled and generally unkempt."

"Nonsense," Meg said. "You couldn't look unkempt if you tried. Come on in. Do you have luggage in the trunk?"

"Yes, but for now, I'll grab my little case in the back seat. It has everything I'll need for this evening." Lindsay looked around, the sky was going into a deep blue with touches of lavender and, in the distance at the horizon, a glimpse of an end-of-the-day- sun was casting a liquid gold touch to the ocean. "It's so wonderful here, Meg. No wonder you chose to make this place your home."

"Yes, well after my sweet Admiral left this amazing earth, I wanted to remain where he and I had decided to settle. I like it here very much. I've met some wonderful people and you'll meet them too. I have a very good feeling about Cliff Point being as good for you as it has been for me."

Lindsay smiled as they made their way into Meg's gracious home, aglow with welcoming lights and Victorian style furnishings.

"This is beautiful, Meg," Lindsay said as she looked first at the entryway which faced a curved staircase and then as they walked into the parlor, a room dressed in shades of gold and sage green. A large bay window overlooked the slight hill down to the road and the sea.

"This house is old like me," Meg said.

Lindsay placed her small case down, slipped out of her hip length jacket, and turned to Meg. "You look wonderful. I wouldn't classify you as old at all."

"You're a very well brought up young woman. The last time you saw me, this curly mop of hair was light brown. Look at it now. Gray. Some white even, but mostly gray. But, who cares? I'm healthy and glad to be enjoying each day. I can't complain about my age when some people, like your dear parents and your husband, didn't have the privilege of growing older."

Lindsay nodded. "I know. That's the frightening part of life, it's so fragile."

Meg looked at the sad expression on Lindsay's face as her eyes went to the even and warm flames in the hearth. "We're not going to focus on the fragility. We're going to focus on new beginnings, never postponing joy. I think we're going to have a great time together, Honey. I loved your mom and dad so much, and I have a deep feeling in this old gut that they're smiling down at us right now."

Lindsay turned from the hearth's glow to Meg's very cute face and spunky attitude. "I'm ready for this," she said.

Meg nodded as a plump woman with gray-blonde hair entered the room carrying a tea tray which she placed down on a low oval table in the center of the room. "And this, my dear Lindsay, is Mary. Mary this is my little Lindsay."

Mary and Lindsay smiled at one another as they each offered their greetings. "Mary," Meg continued, "ensures the comfort of this old place, for which I am eternally grateful. She makes the best scones and chicken and dumplings you'll ever eat. We'll put some meat on her bones, won't we Mary?"

"I like to cook," she said, "if there's something special you'd like, Lindsay, tell me and I'll do my best to make it for you."

"That sounds wonderful, Mary. Thank you."

The pleasant woman asked Meg if there was anything else she'd like before dinner then left the room leaving the two women to talk.

"Have some tea, Dear. Dinner will be ready in an hour or so. That'll give you time to change the clothes you're so concerned about, or even to take a nice warm bath if you'd like." Meg poured two cups of tea and passed one of them to Lindsay. "Milk and sugar?" she asked.

"No, thank you. Just black is the way I like it. Dad was a coffee drinker, but Mom and I liked our tea. Not that I don't drink coffee, I like that too, it's just that there's something soothing about tea."

Meg sat back against the pillows of a sofa facing another sofa where Lindsay was seated. "Was it terrible for you after Peter died?"

Lindsay nodded. "It's been terrible since Mom and Dad died," she said. "The whole world changed for me. Aunt Rose and Uncle John were amazing; they did everything they could think of to make my life happy, but it simply wasn't possible. I told them everything was good. I knew they couldn't bring my parents back, but inside, I was sinking. It took years for me to accept what had happened. I returned to the house in Cambridge during college and then, of course, lived there with Peter. He wanted us to stay there."

"What about you, Honey? Did you want to stay there?"

Lindsay shifted in her seat, carefully balancing her tea cup and saucer. "No. I wanted to move on. The house was wonderful, but I wanted to have a new start – kids, a big yard, and a pet or two."

"What about Peter? Didn't he want those things?"

Lindsay took a sip of her tea then placed the cup and saucer on the tea tray.

"Peter wanted success more than anything. He was incredibly bright, but impatient. He had read all sorts of papers written on Mom and Dad and he wanted to be them. A house with a yard, the kids and the pets, they didn't figure into his plans."

Meg smiled and shook her head. "Did he indicate before you married that he preferred not to have a family?"

"Never - in fact when I talked of how much I wanted that, he'd acknowledge my words with a nod and say nothing. I've thought many times that it was as much my fault as his that we weren't a good fit. I should have asked him point blank about the future, but I didn't."

"I was so sorry not to have made it to your wedding. My sister was very ill at that time and I needed to be with her in Colorado; I know you understood about that. How long has it been now, a year since Peter's accident?"

Lindsay nodded. "Just over a year. It still seems impossible. I don't think I would have stayed with Peter - it wasn't working. I made the mistake of thinking that since he wanted me so much, I could possibly regain the comfort I'd known with my parents. I wanted that full circle of family and Peter was enthusiastic. I was wrong thinking we were going to be good for one another."

"I'm sorry," Meg said. "I could tell by your letters and phone calls, more by what you didn't say than what you said, that your marriage wasn't what you'd hoped for."

Lindsay stood and walked to the hearth just a few feet away, then turned to smile at Meg. "It's okay. I think the world lost a wonderful attorney, but unlike you losing a beloved husband, I feel like I lost an acquaintance. I'd been looking at apartments for a few months. I'd decided that if it was so important to him to live in Mom and Dad's place, I'd let him and I'd move on. When that car crashed into his, I felt very guilt ridden about the plans I'd thought of to go on without him."

"And now?" Meg asked with her cup held just above its saucer.

"And now I'm sad, sad about everything, but ready to make a new start."

"What did you do after he died?"

"I spent a couple of weeks with Aunt Rose and Uncle John before returning to Cambridge. Peter's family took some of his books and diplomas from schools and I gave his clothing to charities. Eventually I went back to work in the research department of the law school. I filled my days and nights with long hours of work - I kept busy. I saw very little of the friends Peter and I had known, and I dated no one. People were nice enough to ask, but I wasn't ready. I'm still not ready for that. When you invited me here, I didn't even consider it at first, but then I kept thinking about it and the whole idea of moving to Maine began to have great appeal. I'm so thankful for your friendship, Meg."

"Well, I'm thankful for you as well. I have friends here, Navy officers and their wives I've known for years, and local folks, like Mary. Many of the Navy people retired here as Mike and I did because it's such a gorgeous place and the base here is very accommodating. I enjoy socializing with military folks; they understand how life can be moving about from one place to another. But Caroline and Bill Heddon were two of my dearest friends. When I left Boston thirty-three years ago to marry Mike, I was nearly forty. Your folks were in their twenties, but the years didn't matter, we got along like bread and jam. I taught in the school where they were students, and I lived in the same building before they bought that nice old house." Meg smiled. "They cherished you, Lindsay, and I will cherish you too. If I'd ever been lucky enough to have a child, I'd have wished for one just like you. I know you're tired. I'll walk upstairs with you and show you to your room. You have your own bathroom, so feel free to take a soaker if you want to. Mary has cooked a nice meal in your honor and we'll dine about eight if that suits you. And I have a little surprise for you – you're going to be meeting a dear friend of mine this evening. I'm excited about showing you off."

"It sounds wonderful," Lindsay said, and together they ascended the wide, carpeted staircase of Meg's seaside home.

In her room Lindsay opened her overnight case and pulled from it a soft jersey dress in a deep shade of green. After a refreshing but quick shower, she returned to her room where she brushed her damp hair and applied a touch of deep pink to her lips. The dress was slipped into and smoothed over her hips, then dark brown sandals were fastened in place over her bare feet. She looked around the room to a comfortably wide bed with a pure white spread. The walls were papered with a pale blue background; white roses and dainty green vines trailed over the pale hue. It was soft and welcoming. Lindsay walked to one corner where a small secretarial desk stood. She could picture herself sitting there writing notes to relatives and friends back in Boston. She would write to Aunt Rose soon.

Sitting down on her bed with a small towel, she rubbed at her hair, noticing that as it dried, the little natural wave was there beneath her fingers. Lindsay took a deep breath, stood, then, with one last glance at her reflection in the mirror over the chest of drawers; she decided that she was ready to join Meg downstairs for a meal and more conversation. This life in this house was new, but it was deliberately welcoming and it felt right.

As she descended the beautiful staircase, Lindsay took note of a collection of framed photographs along the wall. One in particular was of Mike, Meg's husband, to whom she lovingly referred to as her Admiral. The photo was of him in full dress uniform, his distinguished look, with a full head of thick hair and soft yet intense eyes. He looked like a man of the sea. Another photo of him was one in which he was smiling from a hammock, wearing a bright colored Hawaiian print shirt. There were photos of Meg and Mike being married, others of them together in exotic locations. Lindsay thought how sad it must be for her dear friend to have lost a love so profound.

At the foot of the stairs Lindsay straightened her dress and walked toward the parlor. Finding that Meg was not there, she turned and began to walk toward the hallway where Meg stood talking with a tall, dark-haired, handsome man - close to Lindsay in age.

"We were just in the kitchen with Mary, Honey. But now, let me introduce the two of you. Lindsay, this is my darling Evan. Evan, this is the beautiful girl I told you about. Come on, we'll have dinner together in the dining room tonight. To tell you the truth, I often have a plate in the parlor by the fire. The dining room is too big for one person. Sometimes Mary and I eat together in the kitchen - it all depends on what each of us is up to that day."

While Meg moved toward the dining room, Lindsay and Evan stood like statues looking at one another. Finally he gave Lindsay a slight nod and gestured for her to follow Meg.

"I hope you know you don't need to fuss for me, Meg," Lindsay said, "having a plate of food in the kitchen sounds homey. I don't want to be a bother in any way."

"You are not, and never will be, a bother. It's nice to use the dining room again. Since losing Mike, I haven't wanted to. I'm glad to break it in again with both of you. After tonight we'll dine wherever we choose: the parlor, the kitchen, or here. It doesn't matter. Now, did you find everything you need, Dear?"

"I did. My room is gorgeous. I feel very spoiled."

Meg smiled as she sipped water. "I remember you having a nice room growing up in Boston. That home your parents had was really something."

Lindsay nodded. "It was. And yes, my room was nice. I loved having a window overlooking the cobbled streets and flower-filled patios."

Lindsay could feel Evan's eyes on her and she tried hard not to return the look.

"What propels a young woman to leave a thriving city like Boston to live in a semi-remote coastal town in Maine?" he asked.

Lindsay met his dark blue eyes. "I think change is good sometimes."

"Was it hard for you to part with the house?" Meg asked.

"Yes. I thought about it for a long time. Once I decided to come up here to you and Cliff Point, it became easier."

Mary walked into the room with a tray full of dinner offerings which she placed so that each of them would have easy access to the food.

"Mary, this looks wonderful," Meg said as she offered wine to Lindsay and Evan.

Lindsay held her glass toward the chilled bottle and agreed with Meg: the meal looked delicious.

"I hope you'll enjoy it," Mary said. "If you need anything else at all, just let me know."

When Mary returned to the kitchen for another side dish, Meg explained that she had pleaded with Mary to join them. "She likes to serve the meal when I have guests - I can't seem to convince her otherwise. I try to make it up to her when she has a visitor though - she insists that I make the best chocolate cream pie, so I make certain to have it ready for her visitors."

"Here we go," Mary said reentering the room. "Can you think of anything I missed?"

"We're fine," Meg said. "It's late; you go ahead and settle yourself in, Mary. I'll pop these dishes into the kitchen when we're through."

"Not tonight," Mary said. "This is a special time with Lindsay here. I'll check in on you in a bit, and then there's dessert - mustn't have a celebratory meal without dessert." Mary winked at Evan. "I know this growing boy loves his sweet endings."

"I'll be sure to save room," Evan said with a smile.

Meg laughed. "Okay, we'll let you take care of us for tonight. Thank you, Mary."

"Everything looks so good," Lindsay said. "Thank you for putting so much effort into this wonderful meal. I'm used to throwing together a grilled cheese sandwich and a salad."

"Nothing wrong with a good grilled cheese and a nice salad," Mary said with a smile. "I'll let the three of you have your meal – I'll check back in a little while."

"This is amazing," Lindsay said to Meg as she reached for a bowl of mashed potato.

"I'm glad it appeals to you. Mary's a good cook," Meg said as she passed a platter to Lindsay, and then a basket of warm rolls to Evan. "Now, tell me what you're thinking of doing with yourself tomorrow. You know I have my volunteer work at the hospital each morning, Monday through Friday. I'll be home at noon, maybe we could have lunch together."

"I'd like that," Lindsay said after taking a sip of merlot.

"And Evan, maybe you could show Lindsay your beautiful home sometime. I've yet to tell her of your architectural skills, but I'm sure she'd love to see that room you added to your family home."

"I'd be happy to do so," he said with his eyes on Lindsay's beautiful face. "That is, if Lindsay would be interested."

She met his eyes and felt that there was a challenge between them, something just slightly uncomfortable. She wasn't so sure that she wanted to see anything of Evan's, but this was Meg's friend and it was appropriate to be polite if not totally truthful.

"Of course," she said, "I'd enjoy seeing the outcome of your design."

"Are you nervous about starting your new job?" Meg asked. "I was very impressed that you secured that position through phone calls and filling out the paperwork in Boston."

Lindsay smiled. "I have the distinct feeling that you knowing my boss had something to do with my success."

"Well, Lorna Sinnott is a brilliant woman and she was enthused about your background, but if she didn't really want you to work with her, believe me, she would have declined my suggestion that she give you a try."

"I'm grateful for the position. And, as for being nervous, I guess I am a bit. I have tomorrow and Friday, and then the weekend before I need to concentrate on work. It's actually exciting for me because I haven't really done anything on my own before this. I went from Aunt Rose's to college, college and Aunt Rose's to Peter, and here I am. I love it here already, it's beautiful. I'll put my best foot forward and go."

"With an attitude like that, you're going to be just fine," Meg said.

Evan chewed his food and sipped his wine as he watched and listened to the two women talking.

"I was wondering if you have plans for the weekend," Lindsay began. "I passed the signs for Boothbay Harbor on my way up and would love to get down there at some point."

"Let's go this weekend then," Meg suggested, "I love Boothbay. It's a nice ride down. If we left around ten, we could get there, poke around, then have lunch and poke around some more. There's a great bookstore there; I always stock up on my reading material when I hit that place."

"That sounds perfect," Lindsay said. "I brought some of my favorite books with me, but I've read them all; they're old friends. I could use some new books to read. I'd love to find some local authors."

"That's the place to go," Meg said. "You'll find everything you could wish for in reading material. I picked up a collection of short stories there last year, written by Maine authors - I think they put out a volume each year. We can look for that. And other than getting down to Boothbay, maybe we'll have a chance to introduce you to some of my other friends. I'm so glad that Evan could join us tonight. I think you're going to love one another."

Lindsay half choked on her swallow of food, but she allowed herself a glance up to Evan's face where she found a smile on his attractive lips. What was there about this man? He was handsome but also slightly aggravating.

Meg continued, "Evan is the son of dear friends from Cliff Point who, like your parents, died way too young. Doug and Amanda were the first people to welcome Mike and me here; they couldn't have been nicer. It was very sad when Amanda grew ill and died - Douglas was distraught. We all knew that he died just two years later of pure heartbreak. We tried everything to console him, but there was no consoling, even to having Evan come home as often as he could. It was terrible."

Lindsay looked from Meg to Evan. "I'm sorry for your loss," she said.

"Thank you," he replied, "and yours."

"Were you unable to come home to be with them?" she asked.

"The Navy frowns on that," Evan replied. "I was on a ship out in the middle of no where."

"He's still in the Navy," Meg said, "but stationed here at Cliff Point until he gets out in a few months. He's been getting started with his architecture career - he's done some local work already. Aside from a wonderful addition to his family home, he has clients lined up. There's a huge project involving a school and attached library further north. He's going to be a busy man when he hangs up that uniform." Meg looked toward Evan and smiled. "Sorry, Dear, I should shut up and let you speak for yourself."

Evan smiled. "You're doing just fine," he said. "You're my number one fan."

Lindsay picked at her food and sipped her wine as she listened to Meg introducing Cliff Point's inhabitants and places of interest. Her hope was that this dear friend would not try to start anything resembling a romantic bond between her and this Evan person. She was not ready for a love interest, and what would be the chances of Meg finding the right match for her anyway when she had so little success herself in choosing Peter?

"So," Evan said looking directly at Lindsay, "Meg told me that your folks were prominent attorneys in Boston. Did law interest you as well?"

"Not to that extent. I worked at a law school in their research department, but I never thought about becoming a lawyer."

"And is this where you met your husband?"

"Yes," Lindsay replied.

"He was just thirty-four," Meg said. "Such a loss of a brilliant young life - speed and drinking are a terrible mix. I hope that driver understands what he's done."

Lindsay said nothing, but she thought about how often Peter had introduced her as the daughter of William and Caroline Heddon, not as Lindsay. It seemed she hadn't been enough without the well-known name."

After moving to the parlor and a pleasant evening of conversation by the hearth, Meg noted with the chimes from her grandfather clock that it was eleven. "You must be weary, Dear," she said to Lindsay. "I usually watch the news, but if you'd care to go on upstairs, you go right ahead. I'm sure Evan would agree with me."

Evan stood as he placed his coffee cup and saucer down on a small table. "I agree completely," he said. "In fact, I need to get going." He hugged Meg and thanked her for dinner, then gave Lindsay a long look. "I'm glad to have met you," he said. "I'm sure our paths will cross again. But," he said with a slight hesitation, "do be careful navigating these streets. Tourists can be fooled by the narrowness and twists of the roads. It can be hazardous."

Lindsay wondered why he would make such a comment; she wasn't a tourist, but she thanked him for his warning then turned her attention to Meg. "I usually watch the eleven o'clock news too. I'll stay and watch it with you, and then I think I will go to bed. I'll get my things out of the car in the morning."

Evan excused himself, slipped into a leather jacket from Meg's entryway closet, and said goodbye as he closed the front door. Lindsay watched him go just a few feet to his car then realized with certainty he was the rude driver in the dark car at the stop sign.

"I haven't seen a car like that one before," she said to Meg.

Meg smiled. "It's English - it was his father's."

Chapter Two

When morning came, Lindsay opened her eyes to sunshine, squinted a bit, then turned on her side away from the brightness to allow herself time to wake up and stretch. She could see by the small clock on her nightstand that it was after seven and knew that Meg would have gone by now to her volunteer work.

When Lindsay had slipped into jeans and a dark brown jersey, she brushed her hair and made her way downstairs and out to her car. She collected three suitcases from the trunk, and then from the back seat, four cartons packed with household items from her parents' home. There were a few items of her own, including more than forty of her favorite books. With as much as she could manage at one time, she made five trips in and out of the house and up the stairs to her room, then spent an hour arranging things there so that it would look as neat and pretty as it had when she arrived the evening before.

With her room looking more lived in, Lindsay decided that she'd love a piece of toast and a cup of something hot: tea or coffee, it didn't matter. She went downstairs and into the kitchen where she found Mary reading the newspaper over a cup of coffee.

"Good morning, Lindsay," the woman said as she stood. "I left you to rest as Meg suggested. I hope that was all right with you. What might I offer you for breakfast?"

"Oh," Lindsay said, "Mary, good morning to you too. I don't need you to make me a single thing. I would love some coffee; I can see that there's some brewed, so I'll help myself to that if it's okay."

"Let me do it for this first morning," Mary said. "Sit down, Lindsay. You're welcome to poke around in this kitchen any time you want, make it like home, but let me fix you something on your first morning here."

Mary poured coffee into a pretty cup and placed it on the table before Lindsay as she sat down.

"This is so much like being completely spoiled," Lindsay said with a laugh.

"You deserve it," Mary said. "Now, what would you like? Waffles? Pancakes? Eggs of some sort?"

"Do we have any cinnamon by any chance?"

"We certainly do."

"I'd love cinnamon toast," Lindsay said. "It was a staple in our house; my father never missed a day without sprinkling cinnamon and brown sugar on his buttered toast."

"Well cinnamon is healthy," Mary said. "But will you at least have some fruit with it? We have bananas, grapes, and nectarines. Any of that interest you?"

Lindsay laughed. "I haven't been urged to eat healthy for a long time. It feels kind of nice being looked after a bit. Yes, I'll have a few grapes for now with the toast. Thank you, Mary."

"You are very welcome. It's so nice having you here. Meg has been out of her mind with excitement for your coming, and now that you're here, I can see the comfort you've brought with you."

Lindsay took a sip of her hot coffee. "You've known one another for a long while?"

"Since they came here several years ago, but it seems like all my life. The moment I met Meg and Mike, there was an immediate attraction among all of us, including my dear husband. We met doing volunteer work: everything just clicked."

"Meg told me you'd lost your husband too. How long ago was that, Mary?"

"Jack died five years ago, and, of course, Meg's Admiral died two years ago. We were like two fish with no fins. We needed one another more than ever when Mike went. You know that at some point the awful separation will come, but I don't think anyone is ever prepared for it. I thank goodness every day for Meg bringing me to this house. It saved me."

Lindsay swallowed a piece of toast, patted at her lips with a napkin then asked, "Meg hired you?"

Mary sat down across from Lindsay and smiled. "Not really. She's the most capable human being, not the type to have domestic help, although she does use a young woman in town to clean the house once every two weeks. That's more to give the young woman a job than anything. Of course, at Meg's age and mine, housework isn't exactly a joy. As for me, I probably would have had to go and live with my daughter in Florida if Meg hadn't asked me to come and live here. I simply couldn't stay in the house after Jack died; it was too much work for me. Meg asked me to come here to live. She said that she was a lousy cook, which isn't true, and that since I was a good cook, and that's up for debate, I could live here and do the cooking to earn my keep. And I dust to keep myself busy. So here I am, and I couldn't be happier."

Lindsay nodded and smiled. "Have you just the one daughter?"

"No, I have three sons too, but I don't think their wives wanted their mother-in-law to move in with them. One son is here in Maine, up in Bar Harbor. The other two are land-locked: one in Arizona and the other in Ohio." Mary shook her head slowly, "Everything changes over time. When your children are little, you think you'll have them forever. But comes the day when they explore and find their own place in life and, as a parent, you can only have the privilege of watching them go."

Lindsay sipped her coffee and thought that the same concept could be applied vice-versa, children watching their parents go, whether to a warmer climate, or to their end. Life and losing could be a challenge.

"You've lost too, Dear," Mary said softly. "Meg told me about your wonderful parents and then your young husband. It seems like way too much for someone your age to have endured."

"I guess," Lindsay said, "we have no promises. It's just hard sometimes."

Mary looked at the pretty young woman and wished she had something more to offer for a positive future. "No promises," Mary agreed, "but there's always hope."

Lindsay finished her cinnamon toast, ate a few grapes, and drank her coffee, then took her dish and cup to the sink.

"Don't worry about the dishes, Dear, I'll take care of them."

Lindsay smiled at Mary then said, "Not this time. I'm not letting you wait on me when I'm perfectly capable. Sit and enjoy the rest of your coffee, Mary. I'll just rinse these dishes, and then I think I'll go out for a walk. This wonderful air is giving me a case of spring fever. I can't wait to go out onto Old Coast Road and sit on one of those beautiful rock forms. This place is like something from a romance novel."

After slipping into her denim jacket, Lindsay hollered goodbye to Mary and left the house, heading toward the right and the more remote area of beach. She was walking along the road before she crossed over to the sand and rocks when a car came dangerously near to her. The horn was blown and the driver looked irritated. It was the same driver, and it was the same car as the one at the stop sign just the evening before. Evan Drury - he could be rude and not someone she was in a hurry to see again.

Chapter Three

Walking along on the moist shore, Lindsay could feel the land giving into the pressure from her footprints and thought how it was very like her life. Yielding, shifting sands, powerless to the inflicted changes offered by chance and by sleepless tides of unexpected events.

She pulled her hair back from her face where wind had swept it across her lips. From her jacket pocket, Lindsay took a length of blue ribbon and fastened her dark hair into a low ponytail. Within moments of slowing her pace to complete that task, she laughed as the wind had its way with the ribbon and she watched as it slid into the surf. She stopped walking to gaze at the sea, then realized that a perfect place to sit was offered to her through a grouping of gray and rust-colored rocks, dark seaweed at her feet. Lindsay sat down, pulled her jacket closer to her body, and allowed her eyes to drink in the amazing sight before her. It was refreshing, rejuvenating, to feel the salty mist against her face, to know the sense of feeling completely in the right place.

After several minutes, she stood and began to walk again when she noticed that across the street there were three small cottages, one of them with a for sale sign perched on its front yard next to one granite step. Lindsay stopped, brushed the hair from her eyes, and looked at that little house with its gray exterior and worn white paint on the trim and shutters. She'd never had a place of her own; this cottage held appeal. She decided to get in touch with the realtor listed on the sign to see about its cost and to explore the interior. With a quickened pace, she turned and walked back toward Meg's house, toward town and the small shops along the main road. It was a charming town embraced with old gas lanterns and well-kept sidewalks.

Lindsay walked past Meg's home and down the street until she came to the real estate office. There, a young woman greeted her cheerfully as Lindsay inquired about the cottage on Old Coast Road.

"That's a great little place," the enthusiastic realtor said. "I'm

Kelly Wharton." She reached out a hand to Lindsay. "Come in and sit down. Are you interested in this property for a vacation home?"

Lindsay sat down and smiled as she tugged at her wind-swept hair. "I'm interested in that house for my home. Now I'm wondering if it's a year round dwelling or meant for summers only. And the cost, of course, I need to consider that as well."

Kelly smiled and placed a document before Lindsay giving all the particulars on the house and land. "It's year round," Kelly said. "There's a new furnace in the basement and the previous owner had the electric updated within the last five years. The roof is ten years old and in good shape according to the inspectors. Everything works. It's a cute little place, but the key word is truly little. Are you sure you'd want to live in something so small?"

Lindsay looked at the information before her and the accompanying snapshot of the cottage. "I don't need a lot of space, it's just me. I love the location, right across from the rocks and the sea. Could I see the interior?"

"Absolutely," Kelly said as she stood and reached for a key. "Are you ready?"

The two women walked to Kelly's car and drove less than a mile to the quaint little cottage. "I love this place," Kelly said. "I'd be interested in it myself for a vacation spot, but I just bought this car, can't do it. Come on, let's show you the inside. It has a fieldstone fireplace, very cozy."

Twenty minutes later, Lindsay informed Kelly Wharton that she would like to purchase the cottage. It met her needs for a new beginning. As hospitable as Meg was with offering her own home to Lindsay, she felt compelled to find her own space. She would buy paint and cleaning materials – it would be a couple of weeks before papers were signed and the cottage made comfortable – a nice buffer zone for Meg to get used to the idea of Lindsay living on her own.

"Lindsay," Meg half whispered when she was later given a tour of the cottage, "I'm afraid you'll be cold here. That old fireplace won't provide enough heat in the winter. Does it even work?"

Lindsay laughed. "Yes, it works, but I also have a furnace in the basement."

"There's a basement in this place?"

"There is. It's not large and the floor is three-fourths dirt, but there is a partial cement floor and a furnace – and it's fairly new. I'll be fine.

I'll have you over for wonderful grilled cheese sandwiches by a blazing hearth."

Meg laughed and hugged Lindsay. "You're too much. I'll tell you what, as a housewarming gift, we'll shop for some furniture. You're going to need a bed and dresser, a table and chairs to dine at, and a sofa at the very least." Meg walked to the thick pine beam which served as a mantle and whisked billows of dust to the floor. "It's a solid old place if nothing else."

"I love it," Lindsay said. "Please say you'll try to like it."

Meg smiled. "I do. I can see the charm of the place. I understand why you like it. I'm just being fussy because I don't want to lose you so soon."

Three weeks later, Lindsay was settled in her new position at the Navy base and home. There were times when she felt frightened at the prospect of facing the future alone. At other moments she felt invigorated at the concept of creating her life without having to consider anything other than her own path. She found pleasure in cleaning windows until they sparkled and polishing wide pine floorboards until they gleamed with a rich, amber patina. A sofa in soft shades of tan tweed faced the hearth, burgundy pillows at each end. An old rocking chair from Meg's house graced one side of the sofa while an easy chair in a darker shade of tweed sat opposite the rocker. The area created a U-shaped seating arrangement, pleasant and cozy. In back of the sofa, Lindsay positioned a small table made of antique cherry and four wicker chairs she'd located in a local antique and flea market. It was one large room with three small chambers to the back of the house: the first room to the far left was a bedroom, just large enough to accommodate a double bed and small dresser. The middle room was a bathroom, and the third room to the far right was a galley kitchen. Life would be lived in the main room, adequate for Lindsay's needs.

At her position in the administrative offices of the Navy facility, Lindsay was gradually introduced to people with whom she would work. Her boss, Mrs. Sinnott, was a spunky little thing with blonde-white hair pulled back into a neat bun, a no-nonsense type of person who was pleased to have Lindsay join her staff. A few young women who worked there as well had introduced her to the best places to eat lunch and told her about the best shops in Boothbay to pick up stylish clothes at reasonable prices. Everything was falling into place – until a stack of alphabetically arranged files on the corner of her desk toppled to the floor. Lindsay looked down at them and then up, startled. Her eyes met those of Evan Drury.

"This is kind of a precarious place to leave a mile-high assortment of paper work, isn't it?" he asked.

Lindsay wanted to pummel him to pieces. That arrangement had taken her more than three hours to sort. She stood and began to retrieve the files and then he joined her.

At one point, their foreheads nearly collided and he removed his hat flinging it in to a nearby chair. With multiple files and loose forms in his hands, he stood and placed them in the middle of Lindsay's desk, which also aggravated her, as he covered material she had been working with. She stood and breathed deeply looking at him.

"I'm sorry," he said as he dusted off his dark dress uniform. "I'm not used to this desk being occupied; never mind filled with….stuff."

"How inconvenient this must be for you," she said as she began to straighten the mess.

Evan looked at her then, without a word, moved to a distant corner of the room where he spoke with Lorna Sinnott. Lindsay noted his large frame and thick, dark hair as sunlight quivered across him from a six-foot high window. He started to turn back toward her and she quickly looked away, back to her files.

As he walked closer to her desk where he retrieved his hat from the chair, Evan stopped. "Heard you bought a house," he said.

"That's right."

"I spent time in that place as a kid."

Lindsay looked up from her work to his amazing aqua-blue eyes. "You did? Why?"

Evan smiled. "An artist friend of my parents lived there. She did seascapes – I have one in my home. For a few summers I took art lessons from her. I'm afraid I didn't learn much, but I enjoyed going there. She was a grandmother figure and she made great cookies."

Lindsay liked the idea of knowing who had lived in her little house, but she said nothing of her own abilities with art. It was coincidental, or meant to be: two artists living in that little cottage by the sea.

"One other thing," he said as he placed his hat on his head, "did they tell you at the realtor's that the place had a name?"

"A name? No, that wasn't mentioned."

"The Gray Gull," he offered, and then he was gone.

Lindsay could hear his footsteps echoing down the hallway. She thought about the name, The Gray Gull. She liked that. It suited the plain little structure and gave her the interest in going home and digging out her paints. Not since before her marriage to Peter had she painted and she missed it.

That evening, Lindsay relaxed by her fire. The gentle blaze was just enough to take the chill out of the spring air as she telephoned her aunt telling her about the research position, new friends, and her little house by the sea. Her mother's sister had been kind to her throughout those lonely years – Lindsay felt a great warmth and respect for the family who altered their lives to accommodate a sad teenager. It hadn't been easy for any of them.

With the call concluded, Lindsay walked to a small cupboard near the hearth where she had placed her acrylic paints, canvases, and varying lengths of poplar on which she had always painted. One piece of wood about two feet long by six inches high was perfect for lettering – *The Gray Gull* would be applied to the board in gray against dark blue. Her house had a name – and why not? She loved her homey surroundings.

As she added a bit of kindling to the fire, Lindsay realized that she was nearly out of oak logs and the kindling too was low. Kelly Wharton had mentioned a man who sold fire wood for the area homes – Lindsay would contact him first thing in the morning.

Unable to reach him by phone, Lindsay drove to his home, an old lighthouse further down on Old Coast Road. That stop introduced Lindsay to Jim Phillips.

"I hope you don't mind me stopping by," Lindsay said. "I love using my hearth and I'm nearly out of wood."

"No problem," Jim said as he bundled logs together and placed them in Lindsay's trunk. "I'll deliver more later this week – this should do you for now. So, I heard you bought the old Gull. That's nice; it'll be good to see the place lived in again. Come on in the house for a minute. I'd like you to meet my wife and our son. Louisa was thrilled when she heard someone her age was moving to Cliff Point. Like you, she was an out-of-towner. Came here for a little vacation – we met, that was it."

Inside the cozy kitchen of the renovated old lighthouse, Lindsay turned full circle. She looked at the curved walls and the suspended spheres of colored glass hanging at different heights from a beam across the room. "This is amazing," she said as a young woman with a long, honey-colored braid appeared.

"Thanks. I'm Louisa – you must be our new neighbor down at Tilly's little cottage. This is our son Ricky, closely followed, as you can see, by Sloop."

Lindsay crouched over to look into the young man's eyes and asked, "Is he a black lab?"

Ricky shyly nodded in reply.

Lindsay then spoke to Louisa adding, "That's right. Kelly Wharton at the real estate office mentioned that my place had been the former home of Tilly McLane."

"Coffee?"

"I wish I could. I actually need to get to work, but I'd love to have coffee with you another time. Did you know Tilly? I heard she was an artist."

"Oh yes. Tilly was a sweetheart, everyone loved her. She was always painting. In her younger days, her work had been in museums. The last several years she lived in that little house, she painted just for fun. We hated to see her go, but she was eighty-nine and had taken a couple of falls. She went to live with a younger sister about fifty miles away. One year later we had the sad news. That house has been empty for a while now. It must have needed a good freshening."

Lindsay smiled. "It wasn't too bad. I'd like to have you see it sometime. I love living there."

"My uncle was going to buy that house," Ricky added as he stroked his dog.

Louisa ruffled her son's hair. "Nothing was definite," and then she turned to Lindsay. "He's not really Ricky's uncle, but we've sort of adopted him I guess. A friend of ours was considering that place for his office, but then he built a room on to his own home instead."

"You'll meet him," Jim said as he washed his hands, dried them, and reached for a mug of coffee. "Evan is a great guy."

Lindsay felt her throat constrict. Did everyone but her think Evan was something special? How could so many people be wrong?

"Well, it was very nice to meet all of you, but I think I'd better get myself to work. Thank you so much for the wood, Jim. I'll look forward to a nice fire tonight, and the invitation stands: come by and see Tilly's house. I haven't changed it much, just new furnishings – I left the walls that soft white – it's soothing."

"We'll take you up on that offer," Louisa said. "Now if only you painted."

Lindsay smiled and tucked her hands into her pocket for her car keys. "I do," she said.

Although Lindsay visited with Meg often, the two had made a practice of dining together every Wednesday night. Over a meal of ravioli, salad, and French bread before Lindsay's hearth, Meg chatted happily about the warmth of the weather and then asked about Evan.

"Have you seen him since that evening at my house?"

Lindsay swallowed a sip of wine then reached for her tea. "I run into him once in a while at work."

Meg grimaced. "I was hopeful that you two would hit it off. Not happening?"

Lindsay poured tea into a cup for Meg. "Not happening."

"Tell me why. I'm fine with you two not connecting if you really don't enjoy one another, but I so thought you would - I'm puzzled."

Lindsay squirmed a bit in her wicker chair and it creaked as if in agreement with her. "I'm not sure what it is. He's just aggravating. He knocked down a huge pile of work on my desk one day and managed to blame me for the mishap. I wanted to commit homicide."

Meg laughed. "Surely you aren't mad at him for an accident. Come on, give it another try. I'd love to have you both dine with me Saturday evening. Can you make it?"

"Yes, I guess so, but shouldn't you check with him first? I find it hard to believe that he wouldn't be out living it up on a Saturday night."

"Oh no, he already agreed to it. I asked him this morning."

"Does he know that I'll be there?"

Meg smiled then sipped her tea. "Yes, he knows."

Chapter Four

Saturday evening, after Lindsay brushed her freshly washed hair, she slipped a light-weight black dress over her head and fastened red sandals on her feet. Her attitude was that she would be comfortable - she didn't care about making an impression; she didn't think he was worth it.

Arriving at Meg's, Lindsay was invited to join her hostess and guest in by the hearth before dinner. "Come in, Dear. Evan made a nice fire for us, there's a little chill in the air tonight. You never know how the weather might turn when you live by the sea."

Lindsay walked into the room, hugged Meg then sat down as her eyes met those aqua pools belonging to Evan Drury. She thought that the chill Meg felt from the air outside could not compare with the chill from being in the same room with this man. He was undeniably handsome, but that's where the attraction stopped. She decided not to like him. It had to be his family that had attracted Meg – it was possible that the Drury's were perfectly nice people who happened to raise an arrogant and unreasonable son.

After dinner, which was pleasant and thankfully uneventful, Meg led her guests back to the parlor. Lindsay was slightly angry and amazed that Evan never once mentioned to her or to Meg that he had been rude on more than one occasion. If he'd been three, she'd have labeled him a brat. As a grown up, he was someone she chose to avoid.

"Evan has just one more month with the Navy," Meg said to Lindsay, and then she turned to him as he sat across from the two women on the sofa. "Are you excited about the change coming to your life? It seems to me that the two of you have bright new lives ahead of you."

Evan sat, one arm stretched over the sofa's back. "I've liked being part of the Navy for the past several years. It gave me time to figure things out while being useful. I'm looking forward to starting over.

What about you?" he directed his look toward Lindsay.

"I'm here to begin again. I like my work, and I love being close to Meg and having my own little home."

"Did you notice the sign she painted for her house?" Meg asked Evan.

He smiled. "Actually, I did."

"Wait until you see some of her art work. She has this ethereal quality to her paintings. They're really lovely."

Evan sat forward. "You paint?"

It was Lindsay's chance to trip him up – she felt good about him not knowing something about her. "Yes, a bit."

There was a heavy silence in the room for a moment as he seemed to digest this information. "Did you know about Tilly being an artist when you purchased that place?"

Lindsay allowed just a trace of a smile to slip on to her lips. "No."

Again the silence until Meg seemed uncomfortable with the brevity of answers in this conversation. "Well, we'll all be happy to see more of your art work, Dear. And Evan, your work is an art form as well – those architectural drawings of yours are nice enough to frame. Have you heard anything about his accomplishments?" Meg asked Lindsay. "Has anyone at the base commented on his design plans for the new senior center/library compound? He suggested that an activity room be added for kids too, a place where they could go to play games, maybe even hold a dance – a teen center."

Lindsay liked the idea of providing a place for the teens. She looked directly at Evan and said, "I've heard nothing of any of this; no one has mentioned a thing."

Evan's eyes scanned her beautiful face and the corner of his mouth moved into a sly grin. He said nothing but Lindsay was certain he understood. She wasn't giving him credit for anything, except maybe being annoying.

"I should go," Lindsay said as she stood. "This was wonderful, Meg. Thank you for another delicious meal and good company."

Evan stood and tucked his large hands in to his trouser pockets. "Did you walk here?" he asked.

"No. I drove my car. I thought it might prove dangerous to walk along the dark road at night – you never know with some of these impatient drivers."

The look they shared was telling.

"I'm sure Evan would have been happy to give you a lift home – he goes right by there to his own place," Meg said.

Lindsay hugged Meg, said goodnight to Evan, and left. Next to her car she stood for a moment looking at the clear cobalt sky with its field of stars, then she slipped in behind the steering wheel and was happy to be heading home. In the few minutes' drive she wondered: He goes past my house? I wonder where he lives.

The evening spent with Meg and Evan was not one Lindsay could forget. For the next few days, she thought about Evan Drury reluctantly. Something about him was getting under her skin. Her marriage to Peter had been painfully lonely – she was not in any hurry to make a romantic connection again, convinced that it was not something in which she had faith. Those tricky little thoughts about having a man in her life needed to be buried – she decided to fight any intrusion to her new-found peaceful existence.

Connected to the administrative library where Lindsay worked with Mrs. Sinnott, there was a long passageway which led to the general administration offices. Three young women, Debra Simco, Kathy Mann, and Tess LeGere, were all single, attractive, and light-hearted. Kathy was a wholesome girl with a long, lean figure and a soft, sweet face. It was noticeable, however, that she seemed to hold little enthusiasm for anything except her family of younger brothers and sisters. Their problems were her problems. Listening to Kathy, Lindsay was tempted to suggest that this young woman get out more on her own and have some fun.

Debra Simco was a beautiful girl with green eyes and short, dark hair. She was full of zest and afraid of nothing, to the point that she was comical.

Tess LeGere was the base flirt. Divorced, Tess had become bitter – revenge was sweet. Her husband had cheated on her; now it was her turn to attract, but then to repel. With pale blonde hair and bright blue eyes, her shapely figure and smart clothes, Tess drew attention. Everyone knew what she was up to and why, and everyone loved her anyway

Lindsay found the three women to be compatible companions, often joining them after work for coffee or a glass of wine at the Lighthouse Lounge on base. There they laughed and talked about various happenings of the day. The lounge was dimly lit, consisting mostly of soft blue leather booths, and low music playing in the background. It was a pleasant atmosphere where Lindsay felt accepted and settled.

"How come you never mention people you're dating?" Tess asked Lindsay as they sat in the lounge one Friday afternoon. "Half this base would scoop you up if you gave them the nod. What's up with that?"

Lindsay raised her eyebrows and frowned good-naturedly. "Could be I'm not interested," she said, "been there."

"Oh, come on. What are you anyway? Twenty-seven, I think you said? Lindsay, life doesn't wait for anyone. Give in. Get over."

Lindsay smiled, "Maybe someday."

"Kathy," Deb said, "you too. You never talk about dating. You're the youngest one of us here. I know exactly how old you are because we had your twenty-second birthday party right here in the lounge last year. What's with you girls? Life is zipping by."

"I usually have to help at home," Kathy said. "Audra always runs to me and wants to be picked up first thing when I walk through the door. I need to help Mom."

"That's not your role in life," Debra said. "Those kids are your parents'. I know you love little Audra, but you need a life too."

"I know," Kathy admitted and then she took a sip of lime soda and watched a few couples dancing slowly to an old Frank Sinatra tune. Lindsay noted the look in the young girl's eyes – as if there was a longing for leaning into someone and feeling their love and support. Or was Lindsay dreaming of that for herself? Uncomfortable with that thought, she sipped her wine and decided that when she got home she would dig out her easel and work on a seascape's sunset. She knew just what it needed: a touch of arrogant red.

"Hey," Debra said with a loud voice aimed at the bar, "Ted McNee, come on over here and sit with us."

Lindsay looked toward the bar and was startled to see two officers turning on their bar stools, standing and now heading for the booth. One of them was Lt. Evan Drury.

"Ted," Debra began as the men approached them, "you know Tess and Kathy, but I don't think you've met Lindsay, have you?"

Ted McNee was a sandy haired, bright looking young officer with a winning smile and a firm handshake. "I'm afraid I haven't had the pleasure. How did I miss you?"

"It's nice to meet you," Lindsay said.

Ted beckoned toward Evan and began, "Do you girls know Evan?"

When Debra answered that they did not, Ted began the introductions. When he was about to acknowledge Lindsay, Evan looked directly at her and asked how she was settling in. Tess, Debra, and Kathy looked at their friend as if she'd been keeping this wonderful secret. Tess and Debra moved closer together to accommodate Ted, while Kathy moved further to the left making room for Evan – Lindsay, becoming the center of a confining sandwich with Evan's left arm and leg against her right arm and leg. Lindsay felt a troubling tension, a touch of liking the closeness and hating herself for those feelings.

"I should actually get going soon," Kathy said. "I promised to make pizzas tonight and I need to pick up the sauce before I go home."

"I should go too," Lindsay said as she squirmed as close to Kathy and as far from Evan as possible.

"But you've hardly touched your drink," Evan said not moving.

"I guess I wasn't in the mood for it."

"I could order you something else."

"Thank you, but no."

"Lindsay is a coffee fiend," Debra said teasingly.

Lindsay moved her eyes to Deb and tried to force a smile. Feeling Evan's eyes on her and his body so close to her own, it became almost impossible – she wondered what was wrong with her. This wasn't someone she wanted to like.

"How about some coffee then?" he offered.

"Thank you, but I think I'll get going."

He hesitated for a moment, his eyes on her pretty profile, then he stood and stepped aside so that Lindsay could slide out of the seat, Kathy following. The two girls said their goodbyes to everyone and went out to their cars, each heading in a different direction.

Driving home, Lindsay wondered if she'd insisted on leaving because she was tired or if she simply couldn't stand the close proximity to Evan Drury. The warmth from his body mingling with hers was unnerving - why would she be attracted to someone so unreceptive and insolent? It had to be stopped. She decided to concentrate on warm soup, coffee, and a good book by a blazing fire. If she did not allow sad thoughts from her past to engulf her, Lindsay felt comfortably embedded in the quiet and slow pace of Cliff Point.

While her painting gave her a sense of fulfillment, Lindsay could see that her skills were becoming more acute. Her subject, the sea, influenced her mood. Watching the gulls dip gracefully down to seize her offerings of bread made her smile and navigating the rocks to reach the sand gave her strength.

For some time, she had been working on a sixteen-inch square of thin poplar. The scene was what she saw from her cottage front window. Pleased with the way the green sea against the orange – lavender sky melded together, Lindsay decided to have the painting framed as a gift for Meg. When she stopped at a frame shop one evening after work to have the picture measured, she was startled when she felt someone at her side peering over her shoulder. Was there no place free of Evan Drury?

"Did you do this?" he asked as if he'd been speaking to a child who had left a mess.

Lindsay looked at his angular face, swallowed, then looked back at the framing suggested for the painting. "Yes."

After a moment of surveying he said, "Not bad."

To Lindsay that remark could also mean not good, but she said nothing. Evan picked up a package wrapped in brown paper, said goodnight to the shop owner, nodded to Lindsay and was gone. She breathed easier; annoyed that he could affect her.

Not more than three days later, Meg called and asked if Lindsay could meet her that Saturday at a restaurant, The Open Shell, next to the town wharf. The girls in the office had told her about the great menu there: crisp salads topped with crunchy fried clam strips and flame broiled scallops. Lindsay thought it would be a perfect time to present Meg with the painting and arranged with the frame shop to have it ready. The result was perfect - a dark, rich walnut frame against the pale hues of a quiet seascape. Lindsay felt confident that Meg would like this gift to her, a thank you for being supportive in new adventures.

"You're a soothing sight," she said as Lindsay was shown to her table with a ring-side view of the harbor. "I love that pink color on you - it's perfect for this first real day of sun and warmth."

"Thank you. I don't have much in pink, but I liked this dress." Lindsay slipped into a cushioned seat and placed both her purse and the wrapped picture next to her right leg on the floor. As she considered lifting the package to Meg, she heard a familiar voice.

"Here we are. I hope I chose the right wine for you, Lindsay,"

Evan said as he placed a glass of white wine before her, a martini at Meg's fingertips, and something she didn't recognize for himself at the seating next to Meg. His position was directly across from Lindsay.

"Thank you," she said in what she was sure came out in a half whisper.

"This is wonderful," Meg said. "My two favorite young people in the entire world right here with me. Evan, you're so thoughtful. Look Lindsay, he even had ice placed in your wine."

Lindsay looked at the tall stemmed glass. Ice - in the wine and in her veins - how did he guess she liked ice in her wine in the warmer weather? She took a sip and thanked him again.

"Did I choose the right wine?"

"Yes, it's nice. Thank you."

"And the ice – was that a good move?"

Lindsay wanted to reach across the table and spill his whatever-drink on his crisp blue shirt.

"Yes, very refreshing."

His slightly crooked smile aggravated her, as if he was reading her mind.

"Lindsay Dear," Meg said, "I know that I neglected to tell you why I wanted you here with us today. Evan has completed the work on the addition to his wonderful home and he's taking us to see it. I thought that called for a celebration. Especially since I persuaded him to invite us – I have no scruples when it comes to events such as this – I just invite myself along."

Lindsay's eyes went from Meg's bright little face to Evan's gleaming eyes. When he smiled, Lindsay was determined not to return the gesture of joy. "This addition is your work space?" she asked calmly.

Every time he answered her, it was as if he planned the reply in slow motion. His eyes scanned her face. "Yes, a nice large room for my plots and plans."

Lindsay was lost with wondering how Meg found this man charming. He was deliberately edgy – not exactly comfortable to be with.

"His home is beautiful," Meg said. "Amanda and Doug Drury bought that old place, renovated it to suit them, and made it a showplace. Evan has described the new room to me in such a way that I can hardly wait to see it. With your artistic talent, Dear, I felt certain that this was something you wouldn't want to miss."

"Speaking of artistic talents," Evan began, "are you going to show us what's in that parcel with the motif from the frame shop?"

Lindsay wanted to stretch across the table and strangle him. Did he miss anything at all?

Lindsay reached down for the package which she presented to Meg. "It's just a little thank you for everything you've done to make me feel so welcomed."

Evan smiled as he watched Meg untie and unwrap the jute and brown paper to reveal the soft seascape. He glanced briefly at Lindsay then back at the painting.

"Lindsay Wade," Meg said, "this is outstanding. I will never have anything I'll treasure more. How perfectly beautiful that sunset is, and the waves against the rocks. It looks like the area near your cottage. I love it. Thank you, Dear, this is amazing."

Lindsay felt awkward. After Evan's comment in the shop about the painting being *not bad*, she had the feeling that he was laughing inside. She looked at his face and found aqua blue eyes meeting her own – no sign of laughter.

"Are we ready for this exciting unveiling of your new room?" Meg asked Evan as she dabbed at her mouth with a napkin.

"If Lindsay's through with her lunch - you've hardly touched your plate," he said. "Was the food not something you cared for?"

Lindsay looked down at the attractively arranged salad, the clam strips she loved sitting undisturbed on the top. "It's delicious," she said. "I'll ask for it to go and have it later."

His eyes met hers again and it was as though he knew. She was far from being at ease in his presence.

"Did you walk here, Dear, or did you drive?" Meg asked Lindsay. "Evan picked me up and I'm sure we could all go together, right Evan?"

"Of course," he said.

Lindsay reluctantly admitted to having walked the half mile from her home and after receiving her meal to go in a plastic container, they went out to Evan's car. As she started to move into the back seat, Meg placed her hand on Lindsay's right arm. "Sit up front with us, Dear. There's plenty of room for the three of us in Evan's roomy car."

Lindsay hesitated as Meg slid to the middle leaving Lindsay grateful to be seated by the window, away from Evan.

As they drove from the wharf, passing Meg's house and Lindsay's cottage, the curved and scenic road embraced the varying sizes and shapes of rocks along the shore. Within minutes Lindsay was jolted away from the calm sea to a driveway which brought them to a halt before a large stone house trimmed in white – like her cottage. She found its exterior to be simple yet beautiful. The grays and rusts of the irregular rock forms could not have been more carefully arranged, and the addition in dark chocolate-colored wood shingles created a wonderful contrast to the stone. She noticed the tall windows, curved at the top – no doubt to invite more light into Evan's new work space. She had to admit, the place was wonderful sitting stoically at the crest of a hill overlooking the sea.

As Lindsay sat looking at the details of the house, Evan opened her car door and extended a hand to her. She accepted it and found his grasp to be large and firm, pulling her gently from where she sat. After a long glance from him to her, Lindsay stepped aside as he gave the same courtesy to Meg.

Inside, they were met with an ample entranceway carpeted in a gray-blue - a white painted stairway stood straight before them.

"Isn't this lovely?" Meg asked to no one in particular.

They were ushered in to a room to the left which, as in Meg's home, was the parlor. Lindsay looked at the huge fieldstone fireplace, the pale gold walls, and the ceiling to floor darker gold drapes at the windows. The space was elegant without being over done.

"I'll get a fire going," he said. "It may be early summer, but there's a chill in the air and the fire should give us just enough for a little warmth. And then," he said with a smile to both of his guests, "I'll show you my room. Would either of you care for coffee or something stronger?"

When Meg and Lindsay both declined the offer, Evan tucked kindling between large slices of oak and struck a match to begin the fire. "Ready?" he asked as he extended his arm to Meg.

They walked to a door to the left of the fireplace which Evan opened. He then stepped aside for his guests to enter into a room that seemed huge. The cathedral ceilings were made of dark wood and thick cross beams. The walls were painted a soft white and the floors were matched to the house with wide, pine boards. The windows appeared even more massive from inside than outside, and the stone fireplace was topped with a thick beam mirroring the ceiling's structure. In the center of the room an architect's slanted table and a stool sat on an eight-foot square of white carpet. The only other furniture in the room was a cabinet which appeared to be for an architect's supplies, a small desk and matching chair, and a pale blue leather sofa. Sparse, the room was directly designated to be for work and to provide the space to think – to dream the perfect design. Lindsay could easily picture herself in this uncluttered and engaging environment, painting with the glow of north light.

Immersed in the room's inviting beauty, Lindsay turned when Meg spoke to her. "I think you'd love seeing Evan's kitchen and dining room too, Dear. They were favorite parts of the house to Amanda - she was a wonderful cook."

Evan walked to his table and adjusted some plans he'd been working on. "I'm not sure the kitchen area would interest Lindsay," he said.

"But it would. I love old houses and from what I've seen of this one, it's wonderful."

He gave her one of his long looks and then asked Meg if she'd like to go along with them.

"I'll wait by the hearth in your parlor," she said. "You two go ahead."

Lindsay found herself walking into the dining room which was separated from the living room by double doors painted white. The room was large with an oval cherry table in its center and twelve chairs positioned around the room. The wallpaper was a pale blue with an attractive fruit design and the better part of one wall was taken up with glass doors leading to a stone patio and garden. The doors were adorned with ice blue drapes to the floor and the pine boards were completely and beautifully bare.

The kitchen was directly behind the dining room, separated by a single swinging door. Lindsay was amazed to find that the floor of the kitchen was stone. In the center of the white-walled room stood a rectangular table, thick and marred with age. Two sturdy benches sat on either side. The sink, refrigerator, and stove appeared fairly modern in a silvery tone, and a variety of copper cooking utensils were suspended over the table. The room was sparse like Evan's new space. It should have seemed cold, but it was the opposite. This was a place in which Lindsay could envision wonderfully prepared meals and a quiet afternoon cup of coffee.

As her eyes embraced the bright room, Lindsay felt something soft moving against her ankles. She looked down to see a black and white cat and she laughed.

"Who's this?" she asked as she stooped to pet the cat.

"That's Adele," Evan said. "She more or less adopted us a few years ago. Sara and Ben look after her." He pointed to a door at the corner of the room. "That's their living area."

"You have domestic help?" Lindsay asked as she stroked Adele.

"Not really. They were invited to live here years ago by my parents - kind of like Mary over at Meg's house. Ben looks after repairs and does the lawn – Sara cleans and cooks when I'm around to enjoy it. They have three rooms to themselves, but when I'm not around, they are free to use the entire house. They're family to me. They belong here." His words were firm - matter-of-fact.

On their walk back to the parlor and Meg, Lindsay felt compelled to say something positive about Evan's new room. "Your workspace is perfect," she said.

"With one of your paintings over my mantle, yes, it would be perfect."

They had reached Meg and neither of them said more. As they were about to get in to Evan's car for the ride home, Meg stood aside and asked Lindsay to slip in to the middle. "I'm hoping Evan won't mind stopping at Gerard's Shop for a moment – they have the best home made blueberry jelly and I'm out of it."

"No problem," Evan said as he noticed Lindsay's slightly stunned expression.

Within minutes, the car pulled up to a small shop where Meg stepped out and disappeared, leaving Lindsay and Evan next to one another in his car.

He broke the awkward silence when he spoke. "This is a painful position for you, isn't it?"

Lindsay felt her throat constrict but she managed to shift a bit toward Meg's seat and lied. "No, why should it be?"

Evan smiled and stretched back a bit, his long legs moved forward. His left arm rested on the window's edge and his right arm was placed behind her on the seat.

"You have many assets, Lindsay Wade, but lying isn't one of them."

She could feel his cool eyes on her and his warm body close to her own. She stared straight ahead and said nothing in reply while she hoped for Meg's hasty return.

Chapter Five

Summer months, drawing tourists, were active in Cliff Point. While the rocky beaches were not good for swimming, the sheer beauty of the place offered opportunities to relax and take wonderful photos of spectacular scenery. No one stayed long; there were very few bed and breakfasts and no hotels – visitors needed to find rooms in neighboring towns - the residents seemed to prefer it that way.

Lindsay began to paint more frequently and enjoyed an occasional evening among her friends, Kathy, Tess and Debra. They had a good effect on one another causing Lindsay to laugh and temporarily forget the sadness of her life in Boston – it had seemed empty after losing her parents and emptier after Peter's accident. She had begun to wonder if this was her fate - losing one integral part of her life after the other.

The Lighthouse Lounge was often where the girls ended up for a late night sandwich and coffee or a glass of wine with cheese and crackers. Music played in the background and couples danced, sometimes fast and sometimes slow and romantic. The servicemen stationed at Cliff Point had an eye for the ladies and were not shy about asking them to dance. Lindsay enjoyed the interaction, but if asked for a date, she declined. She wasn't ready.

As she sat one night watching Tess and Debra fast dance with a young sailor, she was astounded at her feelings when she noticed Evan taking two drinks from the bar to a small table where an attractive blonde waited.

"What are you watching so intently?" Kathy asked as she stirred her tea.

Lindsay pulled her eyes from Evan and his guest. "Nothing, just observing the dancers."

"Really? I could have sworn you were watching that guy who sat with us one night. What was his name? Evan something?"

"Dreary," Lindsay said.

Kathy laughed. "What? No, that's not right. No one has the last name dreary."

Lindsay took a few sips of warm coffee. "Well he should – that's what he deserves, the name Dreary suits him better than Drury."

Kathy laughed again and shook her head. "I think his last name should be dreamy. He's so handsome."

Lindsay raised her eyebrows at Kathy and decided to drop the subject. She liked her life just the way it was, free and fun.

"What about you, Kathy? Anyone steal your heart away? I never hear you talking about a love interest. Tess has just about anyone she wants – Debra has John when he's home from college. You're young and pretty, what's happening?"

Kathy shrugged. "There was someone a while back. I don't know; I stay busy with my family."

Lindsay decided to ask nothing more – maybe Kathy had her reasons.

When Lindsay's eyes drifted quickly to and from Evan, she decided this had the distinct feeling of torture. She was tired anyway – time to go home. "Will you tell Tess and Debra I said goodnight? I'm heading out."

"Sure," Kathy said. "Are you okay? You aren't sick, are you?"

Lindsay smiled as she picked up her purse and stood. "Not at all. I'm just getting sleepy and I'm off to Boothbay with Meg early tomorrow. I love it there – there's every kind of shop – clothing, books, groceries; the harbor is so alive – it's great. See you Monday at work."

Lindsay slipped out of the booth and quietly past where Evan sat with his back to her, obviously engaged in an interesting conversation with his blonde. She left unnoticed by him which was exactly what she planned.

On evening, as Meg and Lindsay sat in the comfortable little cottage with an after dinner coffee, Lindsay thought about the fact that her friend had seemed subdued for their entire visit. She waited, hoping that whatever was troubling Meg would be revealed - Lindsay was fearful that it could be an illness.

"Are you okay?" Lindsay finally asked as the two sat on the sofa staring at a dark hearth.

Meg's mouth curled into a half-smile, half-frown as she turned to

Lindsay. "I'm a little concerned for Evan."

Lindsay straightened up and placed her drink on the low table before her. Meg had brought Evan up from time to time, but in trying to keep him from her thoughts, Lindsay seldom commented – keeping him at bay physically and emotionally. Whether walking on the beach or painting her beautiful sea, Lindsay found that thoughts of him crept into her head, and maybe her heart, try as she may to evict them.

"What's going on?" Lindsay asked, suddenly fearful that it might be Evan who was ill.

Meg sighed and took a sip of her drink before placing it next to Lindsay's. "Evan is caught up in something important and I don't know how to help."

Lindsay immediately thought of the blonde she'd seen him with at the Lighthouse Lounge. "What's the problem? Is it something you can talk about?"

Meg turned to Lindsay. "Have you met Keith Hatherly from the base?"

"No, but I've heard about him through Tess and Debra. I know he lost his wife a few years ago and that he is now recovering from a horrible accident."

"Yes. His recovery is coming along, but he still needs to be in rehab. The issue is his seven year-old son, Sean. An aunt and uncle in Missouri, relatives of his mother, want custody. The lawyers are saying that Keith isn't fit at this time to take charge of his son, and there's no other family nearby. Evan offered to take Sean to his home, but the lawyers for the Missouri couple say that it should be a home with two parent figures, not a single man who is still tied to the military. It's horrible. This child adores his father; he gets to see him weekends at the rehab center on base. It would hurt both of them to be separated."

Lindsay sank back into the sofa and crossed her arms over her chest in thought. "Isn't there a couple here who could take Sean for the recovery period?"

"Keith has been a friend of Evan's for years, but he doesn't have married friends nearby. Evan even spoke to Louisa and Jim Phillips about the matter, but they live in very cramped quarters in that old lighthouse. Their own son has a room that is about big enough to turn around in – the authorities would never allow Sean to live there. This is a mess, and something needs to happen soon or Sean could end up in Missouri, away from his dad, living in a place he's never even seen."

"That's awful," Lindsay said, "as if the poor father didn't have enough grief with losing his wife and being in an accident. There must be something we could do to make things right. I mean, it's a temporary issue – Keith will be well in time. Where is Sean living now?"

"During the week at boarding school and weekends with a couple about to ship out. They have another two weeks I think; they're leaving Cliff Point for a base in Virginia. That's no better than Missouri for distance. It all seems so hopeless to Evan – he wants to help, but how? As a single man, he's not an option."

Lindsay thought again about the blonde she'd seen with Evan and with a sickening feeling in the pit of her stomach, she wondered. Could he put himself in a marriage of convenience for the sake of his friend's son? She decided not to mention that as a solution yet.

Deep in thought, Lindsay watched as Meg slowly paced the room. "It's such a tough situation. The boy loves his life, and the school here in Cliff Point is perfect. He'd be able to be with his father on weekends at the guest house next to the rehab center. Wouldn't you think that in this day and age we'd be able to negotiate this? My friends in Cliff Point are all older folks like me. The only couple I know who would be classified as a young family is the Phillips. It's going to be a shame if that child is taken away from his father."

When the evening was over, Lindsay walked Meg to her car and then returned to her hearth's mantle where she blew out two candles. The dispute between Keith Hatherly and his sister-in-law in Missouri was complicated and troubling. She'd heard that Keith was a fine officer and a very nice person – this shouldn't be happening. Lindsay changed out of her clothes and into light pajamas before slipping into bed. It began to rain hard and, turning on her side in bed, she listened, thinking of the heavens and Sean's mother grieving for the loss that could occur.

Chapter Six

It was not more than two days later when Lindsay walked into her home and heard the telephone ringing. Meg's voice at the other end held the sound of urgency and that unnerved Lindsay.

"I'm sorry, Lindsay. I'm all wound up about this thing with Keith and his son, but I may have a solution. I need to discuss it with you. Could you come for dinner tonight? Mary is making a wonderfully fresh salad. Please, Dear, say you'll come."

Lindsay dropped her shoulder purse on a chair and scuffed off her shoes. "Okay, give me twenty minutes for a quick shower and change of clothes. Can you give me a hint what this is about? I mean, I know it's Keith, but can you tell me anything more?"

"Not on the phone, Dear."

Lindsay hurried with her shower and, with her dark hair still damp, she changed into blue jeans and a blue and white checked shirt. She slipped sandals on her feet, grabbed her car keys and purse, and was gone.

Lindsay hoped for the conversation first, but dinner, a salad laced with tiny wedges of watermelon, and warm rolls on the side were placed before her. After the meal, Meg nervously suggested that they sit in the parlor where they could finish their iced tea and talk. Lindsay was mystified as she sat in her favorite roomy chair while Meg sat up straight on the sofa, her hands folded tightly on her lap.

"Lindsay. I'm very apprehensive about presenting this idea to you, so please bear with me. Hear me out - consider my suggestion."

Lindsay smiled. "Out with it. Come on - don't keep me in suspense any longer. What is it?"

Meg squirmed a bit and then looked Lindsay directly in her dark blue eyes. "I think I may have a solution."

"Terrific. What are you thinking?"

"You and Evan marry and file for temporary custody of the boy."

Lindsay's mind whirled – she actually felt dizzy and shocked at the words she'd just heard. "Meg, you can't be serious."

"I know it must sound absurd, but think about it. What else is there to do? Timing is important. If this is going to happen, it needs to be soon."

Lindsay sat forward and clasped her hands together at her knees. "Meg, I can't marry Evan. This is crazy. Have you mentioned this to him? I'm sure he'll go into a tail spin hearing this suggestion. We don't even like one another."

Meg looked suddenly calm. "He's willing to do it if it will save the situation. Keith's lawyer said it could work. It would be natural for Keith's best friend and his wife to take the child under their wing. Evan can't do it alone."

Lindsay stood and walked to the mantle where she looked at miniature pictures of Meg and her husband together in varying locations. She turned and faced Meg. "Why me? I've seen Evan with other women – well, at least one other woman. We are nothing to one another."

"Sweetie," Meg began, "I know what you're saying, but it isn't that I'm suggesting a traditional marriage. The only thing is, you'd need to move to Evan's home. The child would remain at the rehab guest quarters weekends and school during the week - Sara and Ben would gladly look after him if he chose to pay you a visit. But it's really just a formality to look convincing on paper."

"What about Evan's other lady-friends?"

Meg smiled. "I know he's not a monk, but they are hardly the types to display good mothering techniques. And Evan knows you'd be quick to release him when this is settled, when Keith is once again well."

"Great," Lindsay mumbled, "I'm dependable – that's flattering."

Meg looked away and then back at Lindsay. "You know we wouldn't ask this of you if it weren't for a little boy. I know it would inconvenience you, but just for a while, then you and Evan can get the marriage annulled – over and done with – if you want to."

Lindsay looked at Meg in disbelief. "If we want to?"

Meg had the look of guilt on her face and, unlike her, she was quiet.

"Do you really think we could deceive the social worker, or the lawyers for the family in Missouri? I have strong doubts."

"But what would be the harm in trying? We could have a little ceremony at my house – just enough to make it seem romantic. I think it's worth a try. That is, if you're willing."

Lindsay felt bewildered and taken advantage of. She stood, walked to her purse and shifted the strap to her shoulder as she walked toward the door.

"Are you angry with me?" Meg asked softly.

"No, I'm not angry. I'm frustrated. I'm stunned. I'm also tired. I'm going home to think about this mess, but Meg, don't plan on this happening. I need a little time to digest this lovely proposal."

Meg stood and walked to Lindsay giving her a hug. "I'm sorry, Sweetie. I know I've put you in a difficult place."

Driving home, Lindsay thought about how she always seemed to be walking away from an issue. Her marriage to Peter Wade had been disappointing and lonely; she was certain that she would have left had he not died. Boston could no longer offer solace. And now this, a genuine human need.

In her cottage, she thought about painting but could not bring herself to dig out the supplies. She switched on the TV and, although it was bright and people were laughing at the late night comic, she heard nothing as she stared at the screen mindlessly. Was she considering going through with this insane scheme? Possibly. She decided to go to bed – sleep often provided a good escape from tension.

Two days later, on a Saturday, Lindsay was shopping for a few groceries and stopped in to see Meg. She wasn't there more than ten minutes when Evan walked in and interrupted a conversation about him. Words were hushed and halted, creating an awkward few moments in his company. Lindsay decided to leave Meg and her guest when Mary entered the parlor.

"Lindsay, you have a telephone call, Dear."

"But no one knows I'm here," she said as she followed Mary out into the hallway and picked up the phone. "Hello?"

"Lin, I'm sorry," Kathy cried. "I tried your place. I know you don't keep your cell phone on except for emergencies. I took a chance on calling you at Meg's. I'm at the hospital. I need you. Please, please come!"

"I will. But Kathy, what's wrong? Are you hurt?"

"No, no! It's not me. It's Audra! She has a high fever. Please," Kathy pleaded between sobs.

"I'll be right there," Lindsay answered and hung up the phone. Lindsay looked dazed when she hurried back to Meg's parlor. "I need to get to the hospital. A friend's little sister is ill – she's absolutely frantic with worry."

"I'll drive you," Evan said matter-of-factly and Lindsay didn't argue. They made the hasty journey to the hospital in less than ten minutes, neither of them speaking during the trip. There they were directed to a waiting room on the second floor where Kathy stood looking exhausted and hysterical. She ran to Lindsay's arms.

"I'm so sorry to bother you, Lin. I needed someone here with me. I couldn't get hold of Tess."

"It's okay," Lindsay assured her as they sat down, Evan looking bewildered in the doorway.

"Audra has this high fever, Lin. I'm so afraid."

Lindsay took Kathy's hands in her own. "Where are your parents? Do they know?"

Kathy shook her head from side to side. "They're away. Everyone went camping except Audra and me. She was fine last night. All of this just happened today."

"Can you get in touch with them? Shouldn't they know that their baby girl is sick?"

"I tried calling them. They must be in an area where the cell doesn't work. But Lin, Audra is my baby! She's mine! I can't lose her – I can't!" Kathy leaned toward Lindsay and sobbed again.

So this was it, the reason why Kathy was so devoted to getting home evenings to her family, to her little girl. Lindsay looked up at Evan's face which reflected a tender concern as she reached for and gave Kathy a tissue. Lindsay stood and walked to him. "Would you mind staying with her for a few minutes? I'd like to see if I can speak to the doctor."

Evan stuffed his hands in his trouser pockets. "Sure, go ahead."

Lindsay managed to find the pediatrician on duty who assured her that Audra was comfortable but that test results were not yet available. He gave an order for a mild sedative to be given to Kathy and she was invited to rest on a cot placed next to the child's bed. Returning to the waiting room, Lindsay found Evan sitting, staring at his cup of black coffee.

"How is she?" he asked. "Both of them – is the little girl all right?"

Lindsay sat down across from him. "The tests aren't back, but Audra is resting and they've put a cot in her room for Kathy. I'm going to hang around here for a while. Thank you, Evan. It was helpful having you drive me here. I was pretty unnerved hearing Kathy's anxious voice."

He looked at Lindsay for a long time. "I'll stay with you," he said.

Lindsay was touched. Maybe he wasn't so bad after all. "No, really, I'll be fine. I'll let you and Meg know when I hear something from the doctor."

"Okay," he said as he stood and tossed the coffee cup into the trash. "But call me when you're ready to leave. I'll pick you up and take you back to your car at Meg's. And if there's anything I can do before then, just let me know."

"Thank you," she said, "I will."

When he walked out of the waiting room and down the hall, Lindsay watched his lanky form moving away from her. She turned and walked to the room where Kathy slept next to her daughter - she watched them sleeping peacefully as she sat down in a comfortable chair.

Hours later the pediatrician walked into the room where Audra slept. Kathy stirred and then sat upright, staring at the young doctor for answers.

"Your daughter," he said, "has a kidney infection. We have her on some pretty good stuff for medication – she'll be fine." He smiled and patted Kathy's hand. "How are you doing? Moms need to take care of themselves too you know."

Kathy rubbed her eyes and swung her legs to the floor. "I'm good - knowing that Audra is going to be okay means everything to me. Thank you, Doctor."

Lindsay thought she detected an interest in Kathy from the young pediatrician. They were both tall, slim, and sweet looking – an attractive couple. When he excused himself saying that he'd be back soon to check on Audra, Lindsay moved closer to Kathy and took her hand.

"Are you really okay? I was thinking you might like a cup of coffee and a muffin or something. I can go get you a sandwich, soup, anything you'd like."

Kathy shook her head. "Not right now," she said. "But, Lin, thank you. I'm so sorry to have burdened you with my secret. Tess is the only one who knows about Audra other than you. Mom thought I should let them raise her. I'm never sure what to do except to love her. She's so important to me."

Lindsay sat quietly, then after several minutes she asked again if Kathy would like something to eat or drink.

"I'll get something in a while. You go home, Lindsay. I must have dragged you away from something – I'm so glad I had you with me."

"I'll stay; I have nothing urgent going on."

"No," Kathy said as she stood and stretched. "Go, Lin. I am eternally grateful for you being here with me. But I'm fine now. Please, go. I'll talk to you later."

A nurse entered the room, checked the intravenous lines and Audra's heart rate; everything was fine.

Downstairs, Lindsay called a taxi and was taken back to Meg's house where she noticed Evan's car. It had been hours – she was surprised that he was still there.

"Why didn't you call us, Dear? We would have come for you," Meg said.

"I didn't want to bother either of you," Lindsay said as she moved her eyes from Meg's face to Evan's, then back to Meg. "I'm thankful you were here when I needed you, but I didn't want to tie up your entire day."

Evan said nothing in reply, but Meg asked how the little sister was doing. Lindsay didn't mention the complication of Kathy being the mother rather than the older sister, and it was apparent Evan had been discreet as well – he'd been right next to Lindsay when Kathy revealed the truth. With the little girl's condition explained and her prognosis bright, Meg hugged Lindsay and pleaded with her to join them for dinner. "Evan is yearning for a pot pie I made this morning – say you'll stay – I can have it heated and ready in minutes."

Lindsay hesitated, trying to think of a diplomatic way not to spend the evening with Evan – she was not prepared for the subject of their convenient marriage.

"Maybe Lindsay has other plans," he said looking directly into her eyes, as if inviting an explanation.

More than she could take in one day, she declined. She and Evan were not relaxing together. "I think I need to have a warm soak and a quiet night, but we'll do dinner soon, Meg, I promise."

Virginia Young

In the comfort of her Gray Gull cottage, Lindsay found silence and solitude refreshing, even though escaping the subject of marriage to Evan was impossible.

Chapter Seven

The following few days Lindsay thought about Kathy and her little daughter frequently. She visited the hospital, more to comfort Kathy, since to Audra Lindsay was a stranger. As the little girl improved, Lindsay thought about the father. Kathy had not explained the circumstances, but Lindsay imagined a young serviceman who had entered Kathy's young life and left with a piece of her heart.

Lindsay thought too of Keith Hatherly and his son. She wanted to turn away from the situation, but something inside of her begged for release; she recognized it as compassion. She decided to visit Meg, walking there via the beach.

Wearing red shorts and sandals with a sleeveless white shirt, Lindsay enjoyed allowing the sea breeze to toss her hair, mingling it with a salty mist. She thought as she walked, finding consolation in the ever present sounds - surf bursting against the rocks, gulls dipping and soaring with their piercing cries. She wondered how she would approach the subject of marrying Evan Drury for the sake of Keith and his boy. It would be awkward. Lindsay walked closer to the water's edge, removed her sandals and held them in her right hand as she walked in the water up to her ankles. She looked up at her location and found herself diagonally across the street from Meg's pretty house. As she made her way across rocks toward the street, she glanced up at the sky. The sun, as if not yet born, concealed itself behind an immense gray-blue cloud. Lindsay felt a momentary loneliness. She thought about her own parents and then she thought about Keith Hatherly and his child. It was all such a mess.

After scanning the sky and gazing down at the horizon, Lindsay slipped her sandals back on and made her way up along the rocks to Meg's house.

"You walked here?" Meg asked when she found no sign of Lindsay's car.

"Yes, I did. It was an exhilarating walk and the best place for me to do some thinking."

"Well, you're young, but it still seems a long way. Come on in, Dear. Mary's gone off to church, but I'll grab us some coffee. Sit down and relax – I'll just be a minute."

Lindsay walked around the room slowly, noticing more acutely than ever before Meg's collection of figurines, so dainty and decorative. She thought about her own collection, an array of ironstone, mostly cream pitchers, still packed away. They would make an appearance soon, maybe on her mantle or a small hutch.

Meg walked back into the room with a tray of coffee, cream, sugar, and tiny Madeleines. "Mary made these fattening little things yesterday. Thought you might like them."

Lindsay laughed as she sat down. "I like most fattening things."

Meg watched her young friend holding the steaming cup of coffee, her thoughts seeming deep and elsewhere. "So what brought you out on this moody day? One moment it's sunny, the next it's gray."

Lindsay took a sip of coffee then placed it down. "I've been thinking about Keith Hatherly."

"Oh? And have you made a decision? I've been trying not to ask you about it - I know I'm asking a lot."

Lindsay stood and walked to a window overlooking the sea. "I can remember so clearly the court dispute over my future when my parents died. My father's cousin and her husband wanted to raise me. They never had a family and I think they needed me more than I needed them. I hardly knew them. Anyway, when my mother's sister, Rose, told me that I would be moving in with them and their four children, I was relieved. Life can be such a misery for a child in the wrong hands. I would love to be able to turn away from all this with Keith and Sean, but I can't. Sean is an innocent little boy who belongs here with his father – not in Missouri with strangers."

Meg eyed Lindsay, curiously silent.

Lindsay raised her hands in despair. "Do I really have a choice?"

Meg smiled her approval. "When will you tell Evan?"

"Oh, no," Lindsay said. "You may have that honor. That's one task I'll relinquish. While I believe I'm doing the right thing, this is going to be a huge sacrifice until Keith is well - hopefully very soon." Lindsay paced back and forth between the window and the hearth. "I cannot figure out how I got involved in this. I don't want to think about it. Just tell him that I'll do it and why: I'm thinking of the child and no one else." Lindsay turned around in a full circle and finally sat down and picked up her coffee.

"Well, Evan will be grateful, Dear. No matter what your opinion of him, he will appreciate what you're willing to do."

"I don't need his gratitude. I don't need anything from Evan Drury."

Meg looked bewildered. "I don't understand how you two got off on the wrong foot. What happened? I thought you'd like one another so much."

"I never told you. The very first thing when I arrived here, before I ever reached your house, he pulled up beside me and gave me the evil eye because I hesitated too long at a stop sign. Then he knocked down a huge pile of files one day at work and made it seem like it was my fault. The man is rude. He hates me."

Meg covered her mouth and laughed. "That's what the trouble between you is about - a stop sign incident and a pile of files?"

"Meg, you're prejudiced. He's a friend of yours. He's arrogant. I can't stand him. As I told the girls at work, his last name should be dreary, not Drury."

Meg laughed again. "Come on now. He hasn't got a dreary bone in his handsome body. Evan is strong-willed, but he's also one of the sweetest, kindest guys I've ever known. Give yourself a chance to know him."

Lindsay sighed. "I guess I'll have a chance to know him whether I want to or not. What are the terms of this marriage? When does it need to happen?"

"To be effective, it should be soon. And the terms should be decided by you and Evan."

"What will be for Lindsay and me to determine?" Evan asked as he sauntered in to the parlor.

At that moment, panic seized Lindsay as she wondered how much he'd heard of her complaints toward him.

"Evan, come in and sit down - we have cause to celebrate. Lindsay has consented to becoming your wife."

Those words penetrated Lindsay's heart. She had not thought of getting involved with anyone at this point in her life, never mind marrying them.

"Really?" he asked looking from Meg to Lindsay.

Lindsay wanted to blurt out *no, not really*, but she said nothing. She glanced at him and thought he might voice his appreciation since this was to aid his friend, but she found a slight smile on his lips and no words. Meg left for a few minutes to bring Evan a cup of hot coffee. When she returned, she placed the cup before him and said, "Lindsay would like to know how this marriage will work, Evan. She needs the particulars."

Evan sat, leaning forward, his hands resting loosely across his thighs. "Well, it needs to be soon. We'll need to get blood tests and a license. I'll arrange for that. Ideally, this wedding should take place by next week." He glanced at Lindsay for a reaction – there was none. "Are you okay with that?" he asked her.

Lindsay was horrified to hear herself saying, "Yes."

On the day of her wedding, Lindsay thought about the glamorous wedding to Peter Wade versus the somber, plain wedding to Evan Drury. The Justice of Peace was brought to Meg's home and, wearing a simple pale blue suit and a pair of white sandals with a two-inch heel, Lindsay walked in to the parlor where Evan stood in his dress uniform. He looked confident – Lindsay felt frightened. Evan turned and reached for a clear box on Meg's mantle then took a few steps forward to place it in Lindsay's hands. She opened the box to a six-inch diameter nosegay of perfect little white orchids. As she stared at the delicate flowers, he took them from her and fastened them with a pin to the lapel of her suit. He stepped back to his place by the hearth and Lindsay joined him there for the ceremony. When it was time for the golden ring, Evan produced a beautifully carved band which he slipped on to her finger. That done, he asked Meg to give Lindsay the ring she would place on his finger – it was a perfect match to her own.

"That's it," Evan said when the official part of the wedding was over.

Lindsay looked at Meg and thought how Evan's brief statement was certainly direct and unromantic.

"Well, not quite," Meg said. "I wanted this to seem like a true celebration - a few friends are waiting at the Lighthouse Lounge – they have a wonderful room there for special occasions – dinner and dancing await."

Lindsay's heart sank. What friends? What celebration? She edged over to Meg and pulled her aside while Evan spoke with the Justice.

"Meg, what's going on? I thought this was going to be a quiet ceremony, just us. Who planned this gathering thing at the lounge?"

Meg looked sheepish. "I'm afraid it was me - although Evan was in agreement. We need to make this look legitimate. It will be fine, Dear. It's just some of your friends from the base and a few people from Cliff Point. It will all be over soon and then you can settle in to that quiet pace you hoped for."

Lindsay took a deep breath.

After they arrived to shouts of congratulations and many hugs, Lindsay and Evan were ushered to a long table where at one end a three-tiered wedding cake, adorned with white roses and trails of baby's breath, sat waiting for them. The room, decorated in white flowers and tiny lights, was enchanting. Lindsay thought what a waste it was for this particular occasion.

At one point, Ted bellowed out, "Where's the honeymoon?"

Evan hollered back, "Bermuda."

Lindsay nearly choked on her sip of champagne and then she looked at him, her left elbow occasionally brushing against his right arm. "What are you saying? This better be a hoax."

He leaned in toward her. "We need to seem genuine and, besides, Bermuda will be beautiful this time of year."

"I'm not going," Lindsay said with clenched teeth.

He tilted her head up with his hand and smiled saying, "It will look silly for me to go on a honeymoon alone." And with that, he kissed his wife for the first time .

Moments later, Meg slid into a chair next to Lindsay and whispered in her ear. "When did you two decide on Bermuda?"

"I didn't," Lindsay whispered in an angry tone. "Your pet did!"

Meg looked startled then nervously sat back in her chair and was still.

When the dinner ended and the cake had been cut and served, Evan and Lindsay danced, she keeping an obvious space between them as they moved to the music. Evan kept his eyes on her face, almost as if taunting her now that she was his.

"How about if we say our goodbyes and make our get-a-way?"

"I told you I'm not going."

At four in the afternoon, Lindsay found herself on a plane going on a honeymoon with a stranger – it was preposterous.

Chapter Eight

Within hours the plane landed in Bermuda. The hotel rooms were spacious and elegant, facing the rolling turquoise sea. Lindsay walked about the room which served as a sitting room. It was getting dark outside, but moonlight and torches lit the patio through French doors. A man in a crisp, white uniform opened suitcases, leaving them on a long bench before he left the newlyweds alone with a fresh bouquet of flowers and a bottle of champagne.

Evan stood and watched Lindsay's moves. She walked to the doorway revealing a large bedroom with one king-sized bed. Beyond that, there was a bathroom.

"Would you like to change into something more comfortable?" he asked.

Lindsay glared at his handsome face, hoping that her look made clear her intention to be an impossible companion. "You really have your nerve. What exactly do you think you're doing?"

"Look, the first few days of us being together were bound to be awkward. Being out of sight from Cliff Pointers and the social workers will be easier here than there. The more relaxed we appear when we return in a few days, the more convincing we'll be. And besides, Bermuda is a beautiful place."

"Great. And I see we have one bed. Where are you sleeping?"

Evan sat down on a sofa and patted the cushions. "Right here."

The sofa was short and didn't look comfortable, but she didn't care. Lindsay sat for a few moments, her eyes drifting to the dim and dreamily lit patio. She thought it would be wonderful to sit out there with a cold drink, but that might seem like a romantic gesture. She stood and announced that she was tired and going to bed.

Evan stood. "Sleep well, Lindsay. I'll see you in the morning."

She was not in bed more than ten minutes when she heard a knock at the door. "Yes?" she said.

"Don't be so quick to say yes, Mrs. Drury. I wondered if I might have the use of the shower."

Lindsay lay motionless in bed. This was aggravating. The bathroom being on the far side of their suite was inconvenient. Realizing that she had no options, Lindsay consented to him entering her room. He stepped in carrying a robe over one arm. He did not even look at her as he disappeared in to the bathroom. Lindsay moved to her side, turned the light off next to her bed, and slept.

The next morning, Lindsay woke to hear voices in the sitting room and she sat up to listen. There were dishes being moved about and the delicious aroma of fresh coffee wafted into her room. With a burgundy colored robe over her ankle length nightgown, she opened her door enough to look through to where Evan sat at a small table, a feast before him.

"Hi," he said. "Come on in - we have breakfast."

Lindsay stepped into the room and sat down across from him, looking from dish to dish.

"There are scrambled eggs, strawberries, muffins, toast, and coffee." He held a coffee pot near to her cup. "You like coffee - that much I know about you."

Lindsay held her cup toward the pot then helped herself to eggs, toast, and strawberries. When he offered to refill her cup, she accepted and then stood and walked toward the open French doors and the patio. Looking out to the hues of blue and the pale sand, Lindsay wished she had her easel. She had to admit, Bermuda was completely fantastic.

Evan remained at the table where he read a newspaper, but his eyes were following her too. "When you love the sea, I guess there's never enough of watching it," he said. With no response from her, he folded his paper and walked close to where she stood. "I'd like to discuss our plans for the next few days if that's okay with you."

Lindsay sat down in a patio chair with her coffee. "Fine."

Evan joined her, sitting in a chair to her left. "I thought we might spend the cool mornings seeing some of the historical sights, and maybe doing a little shopping. Afternoons we could spend on the beach or here on the patio with a good book, and evenings we could explore the nightlife in town. What do you think?"

"I think," she began, "that you know your way around here."

Evan smiled. "I've been here a few times."

"With former wives?"

He was still smiling when he replied, "The last time I was here, I was fifteen and with my parents and grandmother. No former wives. So, what about my ideas for while we're here?"

Lindsay swallowed some coffee and kept her eyes to the sea. "I think your ideas sound reasonable." She glanced at him quickly and thought she saw the trace of an arrogant grin; she regretted making him happy.

After a morning touring the island and an afternoon of resting between the surf and the patio, Lindsay dressed for dinner in a knee-length deep purple dress and mahogany colored sandals. Evan walked in to the sitting room wearing a tan suit with a chocolate colored shirt open at the throat. He looked at ease and more handsome than ever. Where they dined, soft music played in the background and couples danced. Evan did not invite Lindsay to the dance floor and she assumed that he simply didn't want to. They were like two well-dressed mannequins, displaying proper manners and making polite conversation throughout the evening.

The next morning, Lindsay was up, dressed casually, and with a piece of paper and a pencil she sketched the scene before her from the patio. Without paints, she took note of the colors in the sea that day, a mixture of aqua, cobalt blue with a tinge of green, and the varying golds and umbers of the sand. It was all so beautiful and she hoped that when she was back in Cliff Point, she could do justice to painting this scene.

When she changed to her pajamas that evening, she could not help thinking of the comfortable yet comical outfit as anything but strange honeymoon apparel – nothing alluring about it. She climbed into bed, read for a while, then decided to pull on a robe and go out to the patio.

"Can't sleep?" Evan asked from a chair close to one of the patio torches. Lindsay enjoyed looking at the way the glow from the flame lit his face and made his eyes seem to sparkle.

"I probably could; I didn't try." She sat down two chairs away from him.

They were silent for a few minutes then Evan asked, "Has all of this been as miserable as you imagined?"

Lindsay smiled in the dim light, her eyes on the stars. "I'm doing fine."

"Yes, I'd say you are."

Lindsay felt his eyes on her but she would not look his way. She found it annoying that at one moment she wanted his praise, and the next she wanted to grab him by the ears and hurt him.

"Do you have any interest in antiques? There are nice shops carrying some English items: dishes, pewter, copper. My mother always liked that sort of thing, and the jewelry here is well-priced."

"I'd like the antique shops."

"Okay. We can rent motor bikes and go exploring. If we find anything large, the shops will deliver it to us and we'll think about how to get stuff home."

"Motor bikes? I don't know about motor bikes."

Evan smiled. "Can you ride a regular bike?"

"Yes. But I've never been on a bike with a motor."

"Not a problem. You can ride on the back of mine."

Lindsay wasn't sure which was worse – driving her own motor bike or having to hold on to him.

The next morning they walked to the street area of their hotel and rented a motor bike for their shopping excursion. At a bend on a quiet road, they found an antique shop and stopped to browse. Lindsay found a nice figurine for Meg and two cream pitchers for her own collection

She had not intended to show him her purchases later that day, but when he asked what she'd bought, she showed him. When they were wrapped again and tucked away in her suitcase, Evan presented Lindsay with a large parcel concealed in brown paper. She unwrapped it to find an easel and a full set of paints and canvases. Overwhelmed and near tears, she murmured a faint thank you.

Evan smiled and said, "I found your sketch of the beach and thought that since I am responsible for pulling you away from your painting hideaway, I could at least supply you with a surrogate set of provisions."

"That was very thoughtful. I've longed to paint since we arrived here. Thank you."

That afternoon, as Evan sat on the patio reading, Lindsay found a slope of land where she had a perfect view. When the sun began to slip toward the sea, she packed up her equipment and walked back to the hotel.

"How did your painting work out?" Evan asked as he left his book on a table and picked up a coffee cup.

"Good. I have enough of it done to complete it here or at home."

"Might I see it?"

"Not yet."

"Oh," he said with raised eyebrows. "Okay, well then let's talk about tonight. There's a place down the street where the food is exceptional and the music is pretty nice too. I checked it out while you were gone. What do you think?"

Lindsay hesitated. "I guess so, or we could just stay here and have dinner."

Evan stood and finished his coffee before placing the cup down on a tray. "This is our honeymoon. I think we should get dressed up and head out for a nice evening. We'll have lots of evenings at home back in Cliff Point."

"I don't have anything dressy."

"Yes, you do. I took the liberty of buying a dress I thought you might like. It's on your bed."

Lindsay thought at first that it was very presumptuous of him to choose a dress for her, but then she reconsidered and thought perhaps it was nice. She walked into her room and found a forest green, floor-length dress across her bed. She loved the color. Holding it up to herself, she twirled around and saw Evan standing, leaning against the doorway.

"Will it do?" he asked.

She hated to admit it. "Yes, it's beautiful. Thank you."

Two hours later, when they stepped into the dining area, she wondered how many women in that room would like to be on the arm of Evan Drury. In black pants and a gray silk shirt, he looked exquisite. They were led to a corner table with a view of the surf – a glowing candle in the center of their table provided the dim light.

"Since this is our last evening here," he said, "I suggest we make the most of it. Would you care to dance?"

Lindsay felt her throat constrict. Near to him was not where she wanted to place herself. "Maybe later," she said.

Evan smiled but Lindsay's eyes were on the other dancers, their hands entwined, their bodies close.

"What would you like to do tomorrow? We'll have until about four in the afternoon, then we need to catch the plane back home."

"Could I take the time to work more on my painting?"

"Sure - you do that and I'll pick up a couple of gifts for friends and hang out on the patio until you get back."

With dinner finished, they sipped wine and divided their attention between the sea and the dancers.

"Now?" Evan asked.

Lindsay knew what he implied, but she evaded the question. "Shouldn't we be going? It's nearly midnight."

"Is your coach waiting?" he asked with an amused smile. "You're scared of me, aren't you? You don't want to dance with me. What are you afraid of, Lindsay?"

"I am not afraid of anything," she said. "Let's dance."

On the dance floor, for one awkward moment, they stood looking at one another before Evan placed his left hand over her right hand, and with his right hand, he drew her close to him from the base of her spine. Without a word, they danced. She could feel the warmth of his skin next to hers; his cologne was light and intoxicating - his grasp was gentle and sensuous. Giving in had been a mistake.

Chapter Nine

Arriving back in Cliff Point, they were greeted by a heavy fog. It was dark, and at the door to his house, Evan fumbled for the key, finally ringing the doorbell - no one responded. "Sara and Ben must have gone out for the evening – sometimes they visit her sister in Damariscotta." He tried another pocket and produced the key, opening the door to a dimly lit hallway and the sweet smell of a much used hearth. Placing the suitcases down at the base of the stairs, Evan stepped aside to invite Lindsay in. He then walked to the parlor and stacked kindling and logs for a fire. "We'll have some hot coffee in here to settle in - unless you'd like something else."

"Coffee is good," she said as he sat down to open his mail. She walked to the hearth and enjoyed the warmth seeping into the room and her bones.

"I hope you'll make yourself at home here," he said handing her a key. "I want you to think and feel that you're the mistress of this house."

Lindsay turned and looked at him, wondering about the use of that word mistress. "What do Sara and Ben think of us as a couple?"

"They're very confidential people – they know the truth. Sara prepared a room for you. There are five bedrooms in this house, two bathrooms upstairs and two down. One of those is in Sara and Ben's rooms. The bath across from your room will be exclusively yours. If there's anything you want changed, just let one of us know. Also, I don't intend to tie you up here as if in a convent. If you have someone you'd like to see, discreetly of course, and out of Cliff Point, please do. I wouldn't want you to think you need to stay in this house every night."

It crossed her mind that maybe it was he who wanted to see someone else.

"Would you like to see your room or have coffee first?"

Lindsay walked toward the stairs. "I'd like to see my room."

They walked up the stairs and a short way down a carpeted hallway before Evan stopped and beckoned for Lindsay to enter a beautiful room with a gray marble hearth. As he placed her suitcase down next to the double bed, she walked to a window. It was dark, but this side of the house did not face the sea. She turned and noticed that a fresh bouquet of yellow roses sat in a pewter container next to her bed. The wallpaper was crisp looking with clusters of yellow and white flowers and trailing vines.

"This is beautiful," Lindsay said.

Evan stood with his hands tucked into his trouser pockets. "I hope you'll be comfortable here."

"What will I see from this window in daylight?"

"The largest part of our lawns and garden - Ben has an arbor and trellis out there where he grows his roses. This yellow bouquet is no doubt a welcoming gift from him. My room is next to yours – if you need anything, just knock." He started toward the door then turned to look at Lindsay. "So, coffee in the parlor in about ten minutes?"

"Yes, thank you."

"Oh, nearly forgot," he said. "There's a key in the lock here – if you'd be more comfortable locking your door, feel free to do so." He gave her a wicked smile, as if that key might be necessary, and then he left.

After coffee and one of Sara's oatmeal cookies, Lindsay left Evan to enjoy a warm bath and bed. She found the bathroom to be large and the claw-foot tub deep and inviting.

Nearly falling asleep in the warm water, Lindsay dried herself and pulled a knee-length pale blue nightgown over her head. She brushed her hair and walked barefoot to her room, then decided that although she was tired, she wasn't sleepy. Wearing a robe, she made her way downstairs for a book or magazine.

The lights were still on – she had no idea where Evan was, but she went to the study where the walls were lined with books. The room made her sad, it was so similar to her parents' study in Boston. Her eyes scanned the shelves where she found several volumes by William Faulkner, one of her favorites. She'd read them all, she kept looking.

"Can't get to sleep?" Evan asked from the doorway.

"You asked me that same question in Bermuda," she said in a teasing voice. "I find reading takes me away – I'm not quite ready for sleep."

His eyes moved from her shoulder-length dark hair to her bare toes.

"I see you have a Michener. Good choice."

"Someone here likes William Faulkner," she said.

"That would be me."

Lindsay did not mention her love of Faulkner's work.

"I'm having a little brandy by the fire. Would you like some?"

"No, but thank you." She started up the stairs.

"Well, would you join me in the parlor while I finish my drink and assure myself that the hearth is safe to leave unattended?"

She felt awkward about sitting with him in her night clothes and tugged gently at the button nearest her throat. To decline his offer might appear to be a sign of discomfort. Lindsay walked into the blue and gold room where the embers' glow was beginning to fade.

She sat down in a chair near the hearth, aware that she had been allowing her thoughts to drift. She looked up to see Evan: his brandy in one hand, his elbow on the mantle of the fireplace. His cool eyes looked gentle in the soft light and she felt an interest in him that she was determined to fight. Just as she had decided to look away, his eyes met hers. There was something special in that look - not flirtatious, it was something between them that was left unspoken.

A feeling of remote loneliness swept over Lindsay and she would have liked to reach out to him, to touch his lean, secure looking hand.

Evan finished his drink and except for saying goodnight, they said nothing more.

Alone in her room, Lindsay lay back against the soft pillows on her bed holding the closed book against her. Evan Drury, my intriguing husband. She fell asleep thinking of him.

When morning sunlight filtered through the sheer curtains spilling streaks of gold across the floor and touching the light marble hearth, Lindsay thought the room was even prettier by day.

Dressed in jeans and a lavender shirt, she went downstairs persuaded by the aroma of freshly brewed coffee. The house was quiet, no sign of Evan. She walked into the kitchen where she found a couple she thought to be in their seventies – the man sitting at the center table drinking coffee, the woman at the sink. They both looked startled when she walked in.

"You must be Lindsay," the woman said with a smile. "I'm Sara

Adams, and this is Ben, my husband."

"It's nice to meet you," Lindsay said as she shook hands with each of them.

"Ben," Sara said with enthusiasm, "this is Evan's wife."

"Good grief, Sara, do you think I didn't know that?" he teased. "Maybe this young lady would like some eggs and toast and a cup of your good coffee."

"I'd love eggs, toast, and coffee – thank you. And thank you for those beautiful roses too – they are very welcoming."

"You are most welcome," Ben said as he poured Lindsay a full mug of coffee.

"It's a wonderful thing you're doing for the Hatherly family," Sara said as she placed eggs and toast on a plate before Lindsay. "It's an imposition – a real hardship for you, we know."

"I hope this works," Lindsay said. "I'd hate to see that little boy separated from his father, living with strangers.

"So," said Ben, "you will live with strangers instead. That's noble."

"Hopefully I'm better prepared for the adjustment than a child. Although," she laughed, "sometimes I wonder."

"Well," Sara said as she sat down with a cup of coffee, "if you have to live in a stranger's house, this is the right one - Evan Drury is a doll."

"Goodness, Sara – I'm sure Evan would love hearing himself referred to as a doll. I'm leaving you girls. I have a tour boat excursion today – I help a friend from time to time; it's kind of fun. It was a pleasure meeting you, Lindsay. Should we call you Mrs. Drury or do you prefer Lindsay?"

Lindsay smiled. "Lindsay or Lin will be fine."

Ben nodded then stood and kissed his wife on her weathered cheek. "Miss me," he said softly.

Ben left the kitchen as Sara smiled and watched him go. "He's a good man. But to change the subject, I want to assure you, Lindsay, that you will be treated as the head of this house. Ben and I take care of all the petty little things here – we love living in this old place and Evan seems to like the arrangement too, even though he could do without us. Our rooms are through that door near the corner, and although we're in and out of here, we don't need to be. We won't get in your way. We're here to help in any way we can. Have you met

Adele?"

Lindsay laughed. "Yes, she brushed against my ankles when I first came to see Evan's addition. She's adorable. Sara, I know that you and Ben mean a great deal to Evan. This is his home and living here for me involves keeping the Hatherly family together. I appreciate your kindness but I'll try not to interfere with anyone's life here. I'd be glad to help with the cooking, however I can't guarantee anyone will want what I cook. I've been taking care of myself for quite a while – I'm determined not to be a bother. Living in this wonderful house is not a burden; I'll miss my little cottage, but I'm going to enjoy my stay here."

Sara smiled. "I might have guessed Evan would bring a girl like you home. I cherish a weekend away at my sister's – with you here I won't feel so guilty about leaving Evan. This is going to be terrific."

"As long as he likes grilled cheese sandwiches, we're all set."

Sara laughed. "Well, don't let him fool you – the boy can cook. He gets in this kitchen sometimes and he looks like a professional chef – the knife is flying through the tomatoes and other vegetables and, in no time at all, there's lasagna like no other."

Lindsay said she'd enjoy a good lasagna and then excused herself to go outside to see Ben's gardens. She found a small stone fountain, trickling softly where birds flittered to drink and bathe, and purple pansies and wild violets lived together in a circular form. Further from the house, Lindsay found a large trellis where roses in many colors entwined together. One rose was yellow and orange with a tinge of red. It seemed that Ben had been making grafts and magic in that garden. It was not fussy, a simple garden, but incredibly enchanting. She thought too of the beautiful bouquet in her room – Ben and Sara were going to be easy companions for the next few months. About Evan, she wasn't so sure.

The front of the house faced the open sea. The living room and Evan's new work space had spectacular views. The wide stone walk up to the front door was edged with border gardens. Lindsay stooped to pluck a weed from a row of white Sweet William and she thought of her wonderful father, William Heddon. She walked to the rear of the house and entered through the kitchen door. On the marred old center table, she found a note from Sara explaining that she was in her rooms and that there was fresh coffee on the stove and a casserole for dinner. Lindsay smiled at the note then glanced around at the spotless room.

Now she wondered, where was Evan?

She walked upstairs to her room. She thought about painting but wasn't in the mood. She thought about calling her aunt but didn't want to explain her name change or the accompanying complications. She decided to pay Meg a visit and deliver her figurine.

"How does it feel being Mrs. Drury," Meg teased as she welcomed Lindsay into the kitchen. "Come and sit down. I was in the mood to bake, so I'm making ginger stars. Mike loved them."

Lindsay sat down across from where Meg mixed ingredients in a large bowl.

"So, tell me about Bermuda."

"It's beautiful there," Lindsay admitted.

"And? Tell me about the accommodations."

"Separate."

Meg smiled and stopped mixing for a moment. "I kind of figured that. And now that you're back, how are you settling in at Evan's home?"

"It's actually not as bad as I'd imagined. Sara and Ben are wonderful, like having grandparents around. And I like the cat, Adele."

Lindsay took the wrapped figurine from her large purse and placed it before Meg. "I found this for you in Bermuda – I thought you might like it."

Meg stopped stirring the cookie batter and wiped her hands on a dishtowel. Revealing the figurine, she held it up toward the light and exclaimed that it was perfect and very thoughtful. "I love it. I have nothing like it – I can't wait to place it among my others."

"I'm glad you like it."

"I wanted to talk to you too, about a party to celebrate your marriage. We invited so few people to the wedding, and we want to make this whole arrangement seem authentic, so I thought we'd throw a nice little shindig here. I haven't had a proper party since before Mike died."

Lindsay was horrified. "Meg, no. Please, no party. It's hard keeping up the pretense; I don't want to have to go through this too often. I'm hoping to lay low for the time being, until this farce can be annulled."

"Well," Meg said as she hesitated in her mixing again, "I know it's difficult, but I really think it's part of the plan. We need to look genuine. A party will be added proof that you and Evan married out of love, not convenience."

It was late afternoon when Lindsay left Meg. Weary, she longed to stop at her cottage and did. Cool and inviting, Lindsay sat down on the sofa before the stone hearth and fell asleep.

Hours later, she opened her eyes, surprised to find herself in The Gray Gull. She stood up, picked up her purse, locked her door, then drove on.

The sun was just beginning to set and capped each wave with a touch of gold. Lindsay felt she could drive along this road forever. When she pulled up and into Evan's driveway, she sat there for a moment tugging at her disheveled hair. At the door, she wondered if she should ring the bell or just walk in. Evan had said to make herself at home – she walked in.

Evan sat by the hearth with a book in his hands and he looked up. "Good evening," he said with a tone which asked, where *have you been and what were you doing?*

"Hi," she said. She felt an apology for being late might be in order, but she wasn't going to offer any such thing.

"I had no idea when you'd return – I've had dinner, but yours is in the oven, probably still warm."

"Thank you." As hungry as she was, hot or cold didn't matter. She walked to the kitchen and opened the oven. The food was still warm and looked delicious. Just as Lindsay would have her first bite, Evan walked into the room and poured himself a cup of coffee.

"Want some?" he asked.

"Yes, please," she answered and then had her first bite of dinner.

Evan sat down across from her. "Sara told me you'd gone to see Meg."

"Yes, I did. Are you aware that she's planning a party for us to include more of Cliff Point people?"

"She mentioned it – does she have a date set?"

"I'm sure she does, but she neglected to tell me."

"Are you upset about this?"

Lindsay pushed her plate aside and took a sip of coffee. "It doesn't upset me, but I have to wonder what possible good this can do. I find it uncomfortable accepting congratulations from people – it's all so deceitful."

Evan swallowed a few sips of coffee. "I don't particularly enjoy it either, but it's for a good cause, don't you think?"

"I just hope it's the last show we need to put on."

Lindsay stood, washed her plate and utensils, covered the remaining food and placed it in the refrigerator.

Evan watched her moving about the kitchen easily. "Do you have plans for the evening?"

"No, but there are several things I could do to keep myself busy. You don't have to look after me."

"What a relief," he said with a smile. "I was just going to mention that there's a pretty decent film on TV tonight – I'm planning to watch it and if you'd care to join me in the study, please feel welcome."

As Evan finished speaking, Adele walked into the kitchen and Lindsay reached down to pet her.

"She's about to have a litter," Evan said.

Lindsay sat down on the stone floor next to the purring cat. "Is this her first?"

"Her first and last," Evan said. "I made Sara promise to have her spayed after this batch of muffins is baked." He reached down to stroke Adele who seemed to adore him.

Lindsay completely agreed – too many cats had no homes. She stood and ran fresh water to fill Adele's bowl and added kibble to another dish. With that done, they walked to the study for a night of TV, each in their own comfortable chair. After the movie, they watched the news, then said goodnight.

In pajamas, she read for sometime then thought about Adele – she wondered if the cat had a comfortable place in which to birth her kittens. She found a spare blanket in the chest at the foot of her bed and, adding a long robe to her attire, she went downstairs to the kitchen. She found Adele restless and crying, as if uncertain about what was happening. Lindsay recognized that the cat's time had come. She quickly folded the blanket into quarters near the warm stove and patted the cozy bed. Adele looked at Lindsay, then, as if to indicate her appreciation, she walked over to the blanket and lay down on her side. Lindsay heard footsteps and turned to see Evan entering the kitchen.

"What's this – the maternity ward?"

"It's time," Lindsay said, stroking Adele and feeling helpless.

Evan knelt down and smiled. "Should I boil water or something?"

Adele stretched out then drew her legs up slightly. Evan reached out and lightly stroked her abdominal area which seemed to relax her.

Lindsay was grateful for his presence. After the first wet little body appeared, Adele cleaned the kitten as if she'd done it many times before. Within a short period of time, a second kitten emerged and again, it was carefully polished by its mother. Evan and Lindsay sat on the floor waiting for more kittens, but none came.

"Isn't it rare to have only two?" she asked.

Evan smiled. "I'm no cat expert, but I guess not." He gently felt Adele's abdominal area. "She doesn't have any moving lumps in there – she seems fine, I'd bet she's done."

"How can we be sure there aren't more stuck?"

Evan laughed. "Well, look at her. She's going about the cleaning up, she's purring and acting like a proud mom with these two – I'd say she's running on empty. If she acts peculiar tomorrow, we'll take her to the vet in town."

The kittens, still damp, crawled weakly over their mother, blindly staggering as she watched.

"I wonder," Lindsay said, "what they are – male or female, or maybe one of each."

"They're a little small to tell, but the calico is probably female – I understand they usually are. The gray one could be either."

"How do you know about the calico?" Lindsay asked.

"We had a calico when I was little. My mother told me they're most always female; and that, my dear wife, is the entire content of my expertise with cats."

Since it was nearly three in the morning, Lindsay wondered what had brought Evan to the kitchen. "May I ask you a question?"

"As long as it isn't about cats," he said as he stood.

"It's about Sean Hatherly. We were married to create a place for him to be – to provide a family. He hasn't been here at all. Isn't that strange?"

Evan reached out a hand as Lindsay made the move to stand as well. "It's okay. Sean doesn't know us that well. He's happy at the school where he's boarded for the last two years. He stays in the base guest house where he can see his father on the weekends. We stopped the process for his aunt to take him away. By the time they figure things out, Keith should be in charge again. Sean knows he can come here anytime he wants, but basically, we're the good excuse for him not leaving."

Lindsay looked down at Adele who was content to be nursing her kittens. She glanced at Evan's profile as he watched them too. Hard as it was to admit, she liked him and that was a surprise.

For his presence that night, she and Adele were grateful.

"Ready for bed?" he asked as he turned out a light.

Chapter Ten

On Saturday morning, Lindsay woke remembering Adele's new family. Dressed in blue jeans and a red jersey, she walked into the kitchen where Sara and Ben admired the kittens and told Adele how wonderful she was. Lindsay smiled at the sweet scene.

"I watched them being born," Lindsay said.

"So we heard. You and Evan must have been up half the night," Sara said as she stood and poured Lindsay a cup of coffee.

"Has Evan been down for breakfast yet?" Lindsay asked as she took a sip of the warm brew.

"Oh, yes. He's gone long ago," Ben said.

"Gone? Where did he go on a Saturday? I didn't think he was on duty today. From what I understand, he has a few more weeks and then he's out of the service completely."

"He didn't tell you?" Sara asked in a surprised tone. "He had to fly to Asia for a few days. I would have thought he'd have told you. It's military business."

"Asia?" Lindsay exclaimed.

"His flight was early this morning. I think he said he'd be gone for a week or so," Ben said, "I'm not sure he knew exactly how long he'd be."

Lindsay was stunned - he'd said nothing at all about this trip. She straightened her back and finished her coffee. "Well, I guess it really doesn't matter."

Sara and Ben gave one another nervous glances as Lindsay knelt and stroked Adele and then her tiny offspring.

On Sunday, Lindsay invited herself to Meg's for dinner. She spoke of Sara, Ben, and Adele, but noticeably neglected to mention Evan - Meg decided not to mention him either.

After work each day, Lindsay went to The Gray Gull where she made tea and painted before returning to Evan's home. With Sara and

Ben retiring to their own rooms in the late afternoons, Lindsay found herself alone, often with Adele and the kittens, for dinner. She thought about Evan and wanted desperately to know when he'd be home. He infuriated her by going away without so much as a word, but at the same time, she missed him and wanted him back. This was a frustrating situation – caring about someone who obviously couldn't care less about her. She was reminded of something her mother had said when Lindsay had her first crush on a boy at the age of twelve. *Loving someone has nothing to do with how they feel about you. Who you love says a lot about who you are as a person.*

Lindsay decided that every day after work, she would make sure to wear something attractive and she'd keep her hair brushed – she wanted to make him wish he'd never gone. She was setting out to be a femme fatale, which surprised her.

The following Saturday, Lindsay went into town and bought a large piece of canvas for Ricky Phillips' birthday gift – his little sailboat needed a new sail and this would be a good project for the boy and his dad. When she'd stopped and spent a few hours at her cottage, she went on to Evan's home and decided to replant and weed the little gardens by the front walkway. She was down on her knees, dirt smudged on her face, her hair wind-tossed, when Evan's shiny black shoes came close to her hands in the soil.

She looked from the shoes to his handsome, smiling face. Trying to be irresistible every day that week, there she was, covered in dirt.

"Hi there," he said. "This looks the best I've seen it in years. Ben tackles a lot of the garden work, but his knees don't work well. These little areas take a back seat most of the time – thank you."

She didn't say he was welcome and she didn't indicate that she'd noticed his absence.

"How are our kittens?"

Our kittens? He had the nerve to use the word *our*. "They're fine, why wouldn't they be?"

Evan noticed the way she answered him in a clipped tone. "Is something wrong?"

She shrugged her shoulders. "What would be wrong?"

Evan didn't reply. He hesitated then walked toward the front door. She could have cried. She had wanted so much to look pretty when he returned, and she wanted something more from this man than an admiration for her gardening skills. She stood and appraised her work

– she'd done a good job. Lindsay loved this old house; it seemed appropriate to make its appearance more attractive.

She went into the house and upstairs where she ran a bath for herself and decided that she would go out – Evan could think that she had a date. It might not phase him, but it would somewhat mend her wounded ego. Wearing a dark brown dress and matching sandals, Lindsay descended the stairs. She thought about the things she did in the name of pride. No one was there to see her grand entrance. She walked in to the kitchen where she expected to find Sara. She found Sara, Ben, and Evan. They each looked at her from head to toe, as if she was a display.

"I'm going out," she said.

"You look lovely," Sara replied.

Evan looked up from the newspaper. "Will you be late getting home?"

Lindsay avoided his eyes. "I really don't know."

"We'll leave plenty of lights on," he said. He did not tell her to have a nice evening – he did not comment on her clingy dress. He seemed apathetic and impossible.

Lindsay called Kathy from her cell phone and invited her out for dinner in Boothbay. With the invitation accepted, the girls walked through the town's pier area, had some seafood, then went to a pub where they player live music. When it grew to be after ten, Kathy invited Lindsay back to her house for coffee and conversation. Lindsay was glad to be able to stay out later – maybe she would concern Evan just a little, but she was even more pleased with Kathy telling her that the young pediatrician at the hospital had called to ask for a date. His interest in Kathy when taking care of Audra had obviously been more than normal.

Sometime near one in the morning, Lindsay drove to Evan's and entered the house. She expected everyone to be asleep, but as she walked in to the dimly lit hallway, Evan appeared at the doorway to his work room, his shirt sleeves rolled back, blueprints in one hand.

"How was your evening?"

Lindsay began to remove her sandals then walked into the living room and sat down on the sofa. "It was a nice change to get out."

Evan walked in the room and sat down in a chair opposite her. "Speaking of getting out, we should be seen together once in a while. The temporary custody claims have been filed – who knows when and where we're being observed."

Lindsay did not feel complacent – she was in agreement. "Whatever is best for the Hatherly family – after all, that's what this is all about." She picked up her sandals and stood.

"By the way, Louisa Phillips called. She extended an invitation to Ricky's birthday party to both of us – I'll be going along with you," he said.

"Fine," Lindsay replied as she turned and walked toward the stairs.

Sunday morning, she woke to the sound of rain against her window. She lay in bed thinking about her life, how it had been and how it was now. Deciding that she gave too much energy to speculation on what might-have-been, she climbed out of bed, dressed, and went down to the kitchen.

"How's Adele and her little ones?" Lindsay asked Sara who was washing a few dishes.

"Good morning, Dear. They're fine. Come and have some breakfast, I've kept some French toast warm for you in the oven." Sara placed a plate of blueberry laden French toast before Lindsay along with a pitcher of maple syrup.

"Sara, I feel so spoiled, but you don't need to wait on me – I'm fine with toast and coffee. And speaking of coffee," she said, "sit down and join me. I'll get us both coffee."

Sara sat down and smiled. "Now who's spoiling who?"

The kittens played at Lindsay's feet and Sara laughed at their antics. "I'll have to find a home for the little gray one. My sister is taking the calico – she's already named her Ginger."

"Has no on spoken up for the little gray one?"

"Not yet. Evan said it's a male. I'll have to see about finding a good home for him."

Lindsay swallowed some French toast and then said, "I'll take him."

"Are you sure?" Sara asked happily.

"Absolutely - I love animals. I'll get him neutered when he's old enough and I promise - he'll have a good home."

"Oh, that's wonderful. What do you think you'll call him?"

Lindsay looked at the energetic little ball of gray. "Charlie," she said, "I think I like Charlie."

Evan walked into the kitchen as Lindsay swallowed her last mouthful of breakfast.

"I've found a home for the gray kitten," Sara exclaimed with a big smile.

Evan looked from Sara to the kitten to Lindsay. "Let me guess," he said.

Lindsay moved uneasily as Sara smiled and said, "Of course it will be weeks before they can leave Adele.

"Speaking of leaving," Evan began directing his words to Lindsay, "Louisa, Joe, and Ricky are expecting us around two. Louisa's preparing clam chowder and chocolate cake – Ricky's request."

It was a distance of about one mile down the shore road to the Phillips' lighthouse home. Just before two, and in the pouring rain, Evan drove Lindsay in his car. She carried the large package of canvas wrapped in bright red with a cobalt blue bow. Evan had no package – Lindsay assumed he would simply give Ricky a monetary sum. The meal was simple and delicious followed with cake and candles, then gifts. Louisa and Joe gave their son a new wind-breaker for sailing and some books, and he received a variety of candy and cookies from Sloop. When he unwrapped the canvas, Ricky was elated and immediately asked his father about helping to make a new sail. With his gifts opened, Evan pulled a small pouch from his pocket which revealed a beautiful gold coin. "I kind of got caught short in my shopping, Rick, but I thought you might like this coin for your collection."

Ricky held the coin, looking at its tall ship design, turning it over and over in his hands. "I haven't ever seen anything like this ever!" Ricky said, "Thank you, Uncle Evan."

Sometime after seven, Lindsay and Evan left for home. It was still raining but Lindsay was thankful for the noise from the windshield wipers – otherwise, it would have been a journey in silence.

Chapter Eleven

On Monday the office seemed unusually busy. Mrs. Sinnott answered a phone then asked Lindsay to pick up her extension – it was Meg on the line.

"I know I shouldn't bother you at work, but I had to tell you – the party is settled. I've heard from everyone I invited and all but two are coming. One couple is going to be out of town, this is a great response."

Lindsay took a deep breath. "When, Meg?"

"A week from Saturday. You'll need a dress, something spectacular."

Lindsay smiled at her friend's enthusiasm. "I'll find something. I'll talk to you in a day or two – right now, I need to get back to work."

As Lindsay placed the phone down on its receiver, she looked up to see Ted McNee.

"Mrs. Drury, I believe."

"That's going to take a while for me to get used to."

"You know," he said, "I can't believe that fox. I never had the chance to as much as shake hands with you and suddenly you're Evan's wife. How did he manage to steal you away?"

"Oh, you know Evan," Lindsay said with a smile.

"Yeah, I guess I do. The women always liked him."

Lindsay laughed. "So I've heard."

"He's a good friend," Ted said as he leaned against Lindsay's desk. "I guess if someone other than me had to have you, I'm glad it was Evan. I had the idea though that he'd be slow to take the plunge – he's kind of a serious type."

Lindsay thought for a moment about how everyone liked him, even her. That was maddening.

Late that night Lindsay found herself in pajamas and robe making English muffins and tea – she'd skipped dinner – annoyed with having to go through a party at Meg's and the pretense of being newly married and in love. Evan walked into the kitchen, his shirt sleeves rolled up to his elbows as usual.

"Hi," he said.

"Hi." Lindsay didn't look at him – she ate her crunchy muffins and did not invite him to have some tea.

"What's up? You seem a little stressed."

She swallowed a sip of tea and looked at him. "Doesn't it bother you even a little bit to be so deceitful? I hate this. Did Meg tell you she has the party all set?"

Evan took a cup from the cupboard and poured himself some tea then sat down across from her. "Lindsay, I don't like the deceit either, but we're doing something constructive for some good people. If we hadn't gotten married, Sean would no doubt be on his way to Missouri. Come on, don't fall apart on me."

Lindsay placed her cup down on the table. "I am not falling apart. However, I don't have to like this."

"I'm sure you don't."

Lindsay was silent for a few moments.

"I was going to ask if you'd like to go to Boothbay with me this Saturday. I need to see a client there and Meg mentioned that you might be interested in shopping for a party dress."

Lindsay looked down at Adele and her sleeping kittens. Yes, she would go.

On Saturday they followed the beautiful coastline to Boothbay and, with a measure of effort, they managed to have some polite conversation regarding the scenery. Evan commented on the sunny sky and then pointed to dark clouds over the sea.

"I love this place," he said as he pulled the car up along the shops. "Look at the way this town was built on a hill – someone had a really great idea here. Anyway, is this okay? I can meet you back here around one and we can have a bite to eat. My client lives in town – I'm doing a renovation and addition for him. You can come along if you'd like. Just thought you might prefer to shop."

"Yes, I would. I'll meet you here at one."

Lindsay slipped out of the car and started window shopping immediately. She found pretty dresses, but nothing she was enthused with. She questioned herself, was it the dress or the occasion for which she could not feel excitement? She saw a set of blue and white dishes in a window and decided that she needed them – at the Gray Gull, she had only a spattering of dishes that had come with the house. She was carrying the heavy carton when it began to rain. Lindsay ducked into a doorway and, as she stood there, Evan's car pulled up before her. He got out, ran to where she stood, lifted the carton from her arms and told her to get in the car. For once, she was grateful to see him.

"What is this anyway, bricks?"

Lindsay almost laughed. "Dishes."

"Dishes? I thought you were shopping for a dress."

"I didn't see one I wanted."

"What are the dishes for?" he asked as they pulled up to a restaurant at the wharf.

"For me, for my cottage. I love pretty dishes and I need a set."

"Okay. Well, are you hungry?"

"Yes, I am."

"Good. This is a great place for fish cakes and clam chowder."

Lindsay was buttoning her coat against the rain when Evan opened her car door and extended his hand to her. She took it and felt a pressure there that was unnecessary, but warm and firm. She looked up and as their eyes met, she felt a chill from head to toe. With one quick motion, he pulled her toward him, then released her as he closed the door. Standing beneath a canopy, they brushed the rain from their coats and went inside. Evan was right – the codfish cakes and clam chowder were wonderful, and after lunch they sat with their steaming coffee and watched the gulls dipping toward the boats in the harbor.

"This heavy rain is going to be pretty miserable to drive in. There's an art gallery across the street – would you care to go? It might help to pass the time and hopefully the weather will break before we head back home."

"I'd love to go to a gallery – it's been a long time since I've done anything like that."

"Since Boston?"

"Yes," she said feeling a pang of sadness. "Newbury Street has some nice galleries. Have you ever been there?"

Evan nodded. "I've been in that area a couple of times – it's pretty interesting."

After a couple of hours in the gallery and browsing in a shop carrying a wide assortment of books, Evan and Lindsay dashed out of the rain and to a café for coffee. There the waitress informed them that the storm was due to worsen and that driving conditions were hazardous.

It was after four in the afternoon when Lindsay sat with her steaming coffee and asked, "What are we going to do? The shops will be closing in an hour or so, then what?"

"I guess we have two choices. We can stay here in Boothbay for the night, or we can try to make it home."

Finishing their coffee they noticed that darkness was moving in and the rain was torrential. "It's near six," Evan said as he glanced at his watch. "I think if we're going to try making it back, we'd better head out."

They pulled their coats closer together and braved the pelting rain to Evan's car. On the road barely out of Boothbay, the rain was coming so hard and fast that the windshield wipers couldn't keep up. Travel was at a very slow pace and total darkness enveloped them. More than an hour on the road and only a few miles out of the harbor area, Evan pulled the car to the side of the road. "I'm afraid we aren't going to make it. Driving is just about impossible. We can sit here and wait it out, or we can try to make it another mile up the road to Tandy House. It's a well known bed and breakfast. I haven't stayed there, but clients have and liked it. We could at least get in and dry off."

"Okay," Lindsay said. "Let's try to make it there."

Evan pulled the car back on to the road and inched forward. Forty minutes later they arrived at Tandy House. Evan ran to the door and was greeted by a woman in her fifties. One room was a possibility – her family was there visiting and the house was full.

"One room?" Lindsay said. "That's a little awkward."

"Yes, I agree, but it's one room or no room. I think we could handle it, and at least we'd be dry and safe. Mrs. Tandy offered us sandwiches and coffee or tea as well. I think we could make it work. Come on – be brave."

Within moments of entering a cozy room with a glowing fireplace hearth and one double bed, Lindsay shivered as Evan walked in with two robes from Mrs. Tandy. The despair on Lindsay's face was evident and Evan smiled. "Just until our own things dry out," he said, "and sandwiches and coffee are on their way up."

It was embarrassing, the two of them in one room with little or nothing on beneath the borrowed robes. After consuming the food and coffee, Evan lay back on the bed. "Aren't you tired?" he asked.

Lindsay stared at the fire, not sure how to respond.

"Lindsay?"

"Yes?"

"Aren't you tired?"

"Yes."

He patted the area of bed next to his long body. "How about getting some rest? I called Sara and Ben and left a message – no one is worried about us out in the storm."

Lindsay sat down on the edge of the bed watching the fire flicker its golden light throughout the room. She turned at one point and it seemed that Evan had no trouble sleeping. He lay on top of the bed's quilt, an afghan over his legs and torso. It was tempting – a warm bed to stretch out in. Carefully, Lindsay lifted the quilt enough to slip beneath it as she kept to the edge of the bed. As she pulled the covers up to her chin, she felt his arm reach around and pull her closer to him.

"You'll end up on the floor if you keep that up," he said as their faces were barely an inch apart. "Now, isn't this comfortable?"

Lindsay said nothing. She turned her face toward the hearth and with the warmth and glow from the dwindling fire, she slept.

In the morning, back in Cliff Point, Lindsay searched through her clothes and discovered a dress she'd loved but had never worn – sleek fitting rayon burgundy – perfect for Meg's party without being too flamboyant. While the front came up to just below her throat, the back was bare to her waist. She smiled thinking of wearing something that daring.

On the evening of the party, she stepped in to silver sandals, clasped a silver bracelet on to her left wrist, and fastened silver earrings in place. She looked festive but not over done. Evan's look when she descended the stairs was thorough but he said nothing until he asked if she was ready to go.

During the course of the evening, Evan clung close, but Lindsay was certain that it was strictly for appearances. He introduced her to the military and town people she hadn't met, each time stressing, "This is Lindsay, my wife".

Dance after dance, Lindsay was ushered out to the floor on the arm of Ted McNee, and once, Tom Whitcomb. Lindsay started to walk off the dance floor after one fast dance with Ted when the music switched to something dreamy and slow. At that point, Evan walked to her and said, "Oh no you don't - this dance is mine."

Lindsay felt herself drawn close to him, his left hand gripping her right hand, his right hand at the small of her bare back. The band leader announced that this dance and song was dedicated to the newlyweds – guests applauded and then joined in. All eyes were upon them and Lindsay felt tense. With the endless dance over, Evan loosened his grip on Lindsay and looked at her. There were bellows and cheers for a kiss; which Evan delivered with a little more enthusiasm than Lindsay thought was necessary. She had to admit to herself, it was incredibly nice.

Back at her table, Tess, Kathy, Deb and her boyfriend sat, applauding the newlyweds. Lindsay found a drink waiting for her. She took several long swallows and then looked at the glass. "I don't know what this is, but it's delicious."

"A gift from your perfect husband," Tess teased.

"Really? This is from Evan?"

"He had it sent to the table for you as he took you to the dance floor."

Lindsay looked at the glass then placed it on the table as she sat down. Had he expected her to need reinforcement after being in his arms?

Kathy excused herself to get home while Deb and her boyfriend and Tess danced to fast fifties music. Lindsay smiled at their antics then walked outside to Meg's terrace for some fresh air. September was beautiful – the air had a crisp chill to it, but it wasn't cold enough to think about a coat or a sweater. As she turned to go back inside, she found Evan watching her from the French doors and she stopped.

"I was wondering if I could persuade you to join me on the dance floor again," he said. "I think we'll need more than one dance to convince the mad crowd that we're devotedly in love."

"And another one of those kisses?" Lindsay asked with a sarcastic tone.

Evan smiled. "Maybe, if you're good."

"I'm glad this night is almost over," she said as she walked toward him and he took her hand.

"Goodness," he teased as his hand was placed on her bare back again, "what an icy little woman I have here."

Lindsay glared at him, but seeing that they were being observed, she smiled and then hid her face in his shoulder. When the evening ended, Meg commented that Evan should take Lindsay home.

"I suspect our girl is weary," Meg said. "She danced just about every dance."

Evan held Lindsay's light evening coat for her and said, "So I noticed."

At home Evan offered a nightcap which she declined. Lindsay walked up the stairs to her room, slipped out of her sandals, and lay down across her bed. In the morning, she found herself still there in the burgundy dress.

Chapter Twelve

Days later when Lindsay arrived home from work, she took notice of the color in the maple trees on Evan's lawns. There was one in particular that brought back good memories – it so resembled a maple in the yard of her parents' home. Lindsay had always loved the way that tree became a neon orange with the tips of its leaves turning to scarlet. This was her favorite time of year, crisp and filled with brilliant hues.

Finding herself alone in the kitchen, a note from Sara saying that there was baked chicken and a noodle dish in the refrigerator, Lindsay instead sliced some cheese and bread, made tea, and decided to have it in the living room. She stacked a few logs in the hearth with some dry kindling beneath and then lit a match to create an even, glowing fire. She watched and listened to the crackling, and as she sipped the last of her tea, Evan entered the room dressed in a casual suit of dark brown.

"Good evening," he said. "This looks nice – I could smell the fire from upstairs. There's nothing more invigorating than this time of year – cool outside, warm inside."

"Yes, I guess so," she said.

"I thought I'd share some good news with you. The courts have delayed any action with Sean – it looks like we succeeded."

"Does this mean that we will now go our separate ways?" Lindsay asked. "Have we achieved what we planned?"

Evan shook his head. "Not yet. It could ruin everything if we jump the gun. Sorry, Lindsay – I think you're stuck with me for a while longer."

Lindsay said nothing – as much as she was anxious to get back to life in her cottage, she also loved living at Evan's house. Being with Sara and Ben felt like being responsible to and checking in with mom and dad.

"I'll be out for the evening. I'll see you later," he said.

Lindsay watched him leave and wondered if he had a date with the attractive blonde she'd seen him with. She also asked herself why it mattered. He didn't belong to her, and she did not belong to him. This was a deal – nothing more.

As Lindsay sat reading with a new cup of tea, Adele walked in flanked on either side by Ginger and Charlie. Finding the three little friends more interesting than the book, she stopped reading and played with the kittens. Eventually the three of them climbed up in Lindsay's lap and nestled close – Evan walked in around midnight and found all of them asleep on the sofa. He smiled then walked toward the sleeping foursome.

"Hey," he said as he touched Lindsay's shoulder to wake her, "looks like a pretty sleepy welcoming committee here." He sat down across from her and Lindsay thought he must be laughing inside thinking about her evening versus his.

"We had a comfortable time together," Lindsay said. "And actually, there won't be many more such times."

Evan frowned. "I don't understand what you mean."

"Ginger will be going to Sara's sister soon."

"Oh, you're right. Well, at least Adele will have Charlie around for a while yet. I think they'll all adjust."

Lindsay sat stroking Adele. "I think it's sad. The mother cat has no say in their offspring's future. I think too many humans think we're the only ones with hearts and souls."

Evan's face reflected a soft smile. "Maybe animals have greater hearts and souls than we could comprehend. And maybe they accept letting go of their young better than we could imagine. I think Ginger is going to a great home – I know that Charlie is, and Adele is the little queen of this place."

Lindsay looked at the hearth which was barely glowing, then she looked at Evan. He had explanations and reasons for everything to make her feel better.

Evan's eyes met Lindsay's glance and she hoped he could not read her mind. She scooped up the kittens and called to Adele as she made her way to the kitchen. She deposited the kittens on their bed and their mother followed. With Evan not far behind she turned and said, "Goodnight, Evan."

"Just a moment," he said, "there's something I'd like to talk to you about."

Lindsay hesitated, feeling that the room was crowded with the two of them.

"Okay. What is it?"

"Have you heard about the hay ride?"

"What hay ride?"

"Okay, I guess you haven't. "There's a hay ride next Saturday night – it's to benefit the hospital in town, a new piece of cardiac equipment. Most of the people I know from the base are going, and lots of town folks too. It's for a good cause."

"How do they fit all those people on a wagon?"

Evan laughed. "They have several. A few of the wagons are part of the historical society's property, others belong to local farmers. There's room for everyone. It should be a fun night. They'll have cocoa and hot cider – no alcohol. At the end of the ride, people can go home or off to a pub or whatever. It'll be fun."

"Wait a minute. Are you saying that you want us to go?" Lindsay wondered if there was an end to all this.

"Yes, I'd like us to go."

"Couldn't we just buy the tickets and not show up?"

Evan frowned. "Now how would that look? Besides, it promises to be a great night. They'll begin at base headquarters and the ride will go for about an hour and a half. After that some of my friends are going to the Lighthouse Lounge for a night cap. Come on – I'm begging."

Lindsay gave him a long look of intolerance. "So, this coming Saturday?"

"Yes - unless you already have other plans."

Lindsay wanted to say that she did, but didn't. She felt that she was living enough of a lie as Evan's wife without adding still another. "I have no other commitments," she replied unenthusiastically.

Evan walked back in to the parlor to assure that the embers were out then joined Lindsay as they went upstairs to their separate rooms.

In the morning Lindsay remembered that she was dining with Meg that evening and went directly there after work.

"How's everything going?" Meg asked over a glass of wine before dinner.

"Good, I guess. The courts have delayed any action begun by Sean's aunt in Missouri, so that helps."

"I knew this would work!" Meg said. "This is fabulous news. Now, hasn't it all been worth the effort? Look what you and Evan have accomplished. You've saved a family from being unjustly torn apart."

"I know, and I'm glad, but what I didn't count on was all the social events we have to attend to seem authentic in this marriage. Now it's something else this coming Saturday night."

"Oh, the hayride?"

"You know if it?" Lindsay asked.

"Sure. Being at the hospital, I hear about all the fundraisers. I take it that you and Evan are going. It should be fun."

"I dread it. Can you imagine me sitting on a clump of hay snuggling with Evan?"

Meg gave Lindsay a sly smile. "I can think of a lot worse positions to be in."

"Well, I can't!" Lindsay said as the two women moved from the dining area to the parlor and a warm fire.

"Come on now, surely you can see his assets. Other than being a fine architect, a patriotic member of the military, almost a civilian, he's just a terrific person."

Lindsay looked away from the fire to Meg's cute face. "He's a barnacle."

Meg laughed. She made no comments, but it was obvious to Lindsay that Meg was hoping for a romantic attachment between her two favorite young people.

Returning home that night, Lindsay found lights on but no one around. She went to the kitchen, stroked Adele softly and played for a moment with the kittens. After checking Evan's work room to see if he was there, she walked upstairs to her room. A good book and an early night would be fine – she fell asleep with the light next to her bed left on.

Chapter Thirteen

In the morning, Lindsay went down to the kitchen before work and poured a cup of coffee for herself as Sara entered the room and offered to make breakfast.

"Not today, but thank you, Sara. I think I'm still full from dinner with Meg last night. I'll grab something later at work. Where is everyone anyway? I came in last night after ten and it was very quiet here."

"Oh, well Ben and I were just in our rooms, but didn't Evan tell you when he'd be back?"

"Back?" Lindsay looked at Sara. "Back from where? He did it again, didn't he? He just takes off for parts unknown and neglects to tell his wife. What a joke - his wife."

Sara looked surprised. "I thought surely he'd have told you."

"He tells me nothing. Where is he this time?"

"Receiving some sort of award as he's discharged from the service. I'm sure he was going to D.C."

Lindsay shook her head. The man was a menace. She'd been furious the first time he went away without so much as a word, but now he'd done it again.

On her short drive to work, Lindsay was annoyed that she felt tears in her eyes. *Tears for what? For feeling left out? For feeling anything at all regarding Evan Drury?*

On Friday evening in her room she felt incredibly lonely. She changed into jeans and a warm sweater – she would go to her cottage for the night. Why not? No one would know or care. As she was pulling socks and shoes on to her feet, she heard voices from downstairs. She opened her bedroom door and listened hearing two male voices – one of them Evan's. With her purse on her shoulder, she closed her door and went down to the hallway where Evan stood talking and laughing with a man in his fifties.

"Lin, this is Bill Lang, a client of mine. Bill, this is Lindsay, my wife."

Lindsay wanted to kick him in the shins, but instead she smiled and shook hands with Mr. Lang. "I'll be out for a while," she said as she took her coat from the entry way closet.

"I understand we'll see you on the hayride tomorrow night," Bill Lang said. "I'll look forward to seeing you again, Lindsay."

Lindsay gave Evan a dagger look as she thought about sitting close to him on the hayride through hard dirt roads and bumpy paths through fields of mown hay. She could not wait to get out of his sight and to her own little cottage refuge. There she lit a blazing fire in the hearth and then took painting supplies from a cupboard. It was at times such as this that she was grateful for the ability to create something bright and interesting – a diversion. She thought about spending the night at the cottage, but after one in the morning, when the fire had grown cold, she placed her paints away and drove the short distance to Evan's home. Frustrated but tired, she hung her coat in the closet then went upstairs to bed in a very quiet house.

Saturday morning Lindsay found a note on the kitchen table from Sara. They'd gone to her sister's for the weekend. It was requested that someone feed and care for Adele, Ginger, and Charlie. Lindsay looked at the dish of food and water – both were fine. Lindsay could see that Sara had left the door to her rooms ajar so that the furry trio could go in to Sara's and Ben's apartment if they wished. Peeking in, she saw that they had made themselves at home on a settee and were sleeping.

Lindsay poured herself some coffee and drank it as she looked outside to the withering gardens. A touch of frost had put so many plants to sleep, while that same coating of misty white added a magical glow to twigs and turf. It was, no matter what the season, a pretty sight. She could imagine Evan's mother standing there at that window watching her small son at play. It was sad, she thought, that they had both lost their parents so young. With English muffins and coffee for sustenance, Lindsay found some gardening tools and went out to pull a few weeds and snip a few of the last roses to bring in to the house before the frost brought them to their end. After a few hours had passed, Lindsay felt weary and sat down on a slab of granite next to a now manicured garden. As she sat, she heard crunching footsteps and turned to see Evan approaching, a jacket slung carelessly over one shoulder.

"This looks amazing," he said, "while you on the other hand look beat."

"Thanks," she said sarcastically.

Evan smiled. "This really looks the best I've ever seen it. You have a green thumb. Did you do a lot of gardening at your place in Boston?"

"Not a bit."

"Wow. I'm impressed even more then. How about coffee? I'm dying for a cup and you look like you could use one too."

"It's the morning's coffee – I make no guarantees about its strength."

"At this point, I'll take whatever. Come on in and join me."

Sitting across the table from him, Lindsay detested the feelings she had when looking at his handsome face. He didn't fill her in on anything, yet he had the ability to fill her up with wanting him to notice her, to converse with her, to touch her.

"You're mad at me, aren't you?" he asked.

Lindsay stiffened her backbone and said that she was not.

"Yes, you are – I can tell. What's going on? Tell me."

"I really don't want to get in to this conversation."

"In to what conversation? Lindsay, talk to me."

"You know," she began glaring at him, "you might consider taking your own advice. I think it's rude and inconsiderate of you to just take off as you do without telling me you're going."

Evan was quiet for a few moments. "I'm sorry - I didn't think you'd care."

Lindsay swallowed and looked away.

"So, do you?"

"Do I what?" Lindsay said.

"Care."

Lindsay stood up and rinsed her coffee cup out, leaving it on a draining board upside down. "Let's leave this conversation at rest. I'm going upstairs to shower. What time do we have to leave for this adventure tonight? And I suppose it's okay for me to wear jeans and something warm."

"Absolutely. We'll leave here around six-thirty – they're getting people on the wagons to move around seven."

Without another word, Lindsay left the kitchen and returned there at six to make certain that Adele and her kittens were fed and comfortable.

At the wagons that evening, Evan asked Lindsay if she had a preference for where she sat.

"Yes, at the rear of the wagon, so that my legs can be down."

"Okay. We'll let the others get on then we'll hop up."

From where they sat, no one could see their faces and they had the best view. At one point, Evan positioned himself behind her and settled back against a small bale of hay. Not more than a few minutes into the ride, there was a rut which caused the wagon to make everyone squeal. Evan placed firm hands on Lindsay's upper arms and pulled her back.

"Can't have you tumbling to the ground," he said in explanation when she turned to look at him with questions in her eyes.

Before she could adjust her seating he secured her gently to him, her body fitting between his legs, his arms folded across her chest. She thought to stir, but finding the position comfortable and warm, she stayed. Lindsay wondered if he could feel that the apathy was diminishing – that she was betraying herself with her feelings for him.

Lindsay relaxed and closed her eyes. During another rough spot in the road, the wagon jolted its passengers and once again, Evan pulled her tighter against him.

"I'm okay," Lindsay said so that she wouldn't seem as content as she felt, "you can let me go."

Evan moved his lips close to her left ear. "I guess I didn't tell you – I'm not ever letting you go."

About to shift slightly from his firm yet tender grasp, Lindsay found her face being turned toward his with one of his large hands, and then he pressed his lips warmly against hers for a very long kiss.

Back at the Lighthouse Lounge for a nightcap, several of the couples found their romantic evening coming to a close on the dance floor. Evan and Lindsay sat across from one another in a booth with two other couples – the distance feeling miles apart. When a slow dance was offered, Evan stood and pulled Lindsay to her feet. Dancing, he held her so close that she could feel every part of his body against hers – she lost her inclination for being aloof – this nearness was magical.

Back at the house, he asked if she'd like anything to drink, wine or coffee. When she said that she was tired, he nodded and let her go.

Lindsay went upstairs and slipped out of her clothes dotted with bits of hay. Lingering in a warm bath, she thought about how she'd felt about Peter. Marrying him had been a solution for loneliness, or so she had hoped. It hadn't been clear until they were married how impressed he was with whose daughter she was rather than with Lindsay herself. He wanted to be the attorney family she came from, the Heddons. She thought too of Evan. She'd resisted him from the beginning, not caring how handsome or successful he was, until now. Little by little, he was revealing himself as someone who was kind, logical, and definitely romantic. With one wet finger she touched her lips and smiled thinking of that saturating kiss on the wagon.

When the water became barely warm, Lindsay let it go down the drain and dried herself, slipping into a nightgown and soft robe for the trek across the hall to her room. She brushed her hair, slipped a nightgown on under the robe, then decided that she needed a cup of tea. At the bottom of the stairs she noted that the living room light was on and that Evan sat on the sofa, his eyes closed and his head back against the cushion.

"Evan?" she said as she stepped in to the doorway, "Are you okay?"

He opened his eyes and looked at her. "Yeah, are you?"

Lindsay hesitated wondering what they were each asking. "I'm going to make some tea. Want some?"

"Sure," he said, "that sounds good."

While the tea water was boiling and then the tea steeping, Lindsay enjoyed petting Adele and her kittens. With the teacups filled and on a tray, she made her way back to the living room.

Evan took the tray from her hands and looked at her with such depth she thought that surely he could see straight through her. He left the tray on a low table and reached out for her hand. The steps to the stairway and up to his room seemed as if they were happening in slow motion.

He lit the fireplace with a match to the waiting kindling and then pulled her to him as he slipped out of his pale blue shirt. Against him, she was helpless.

"You still have time to escape," he said.

She didn't want to escape and her silence spoke for her. Sometime during the night she woke to find herself enveloped in Evan's arms – she snuggled closer to him and went back to sleep. In the morning, she found herself alone and made her way back to her own room. Her mind raced with a million thoughts. What in the world had happened last night? She thought about how unexpected and forbidden it felt – she thought about how wonderful it was and questioned if ever before she had known what it was like to be truly in love.

Lindsay found Evan with a cup of coffee and three well-fed cats in the kitchen.

"Hi," she said tentatively as he looked her way.

"Hi," he said and then he stood and walked toward her, touching her face gently with his hand. "Look, Lindsay, I feel like I need to say this. Last night, well, I guess what I just need to say is that I'm sorry. I crossed every line in the book. I regret letting things get out of control – I had no right."

She wanted to say, but I wanted last night too. I have no regrets. I'm in love with you.

"I promise," he continued, "I won't let it happen again."

He moved away from her, took his cup to the sink, and left the room.

Lindsay sat down feeling numb. Last night might have been a mistake for him, but it would not ever be wrong for her. She loved as she'd never imagined she could.

The intimacy and nearness she'd known with Evan now drew them further apart. He seemed regretful – she felt rejected. It seemed that he avoided seeing her and Lindsay felt too much pride not to comply. She existed, living in his house, which was almost too much to take. She hoped for the Hatherly case to soon be rectified so that she could simply go back to her own cottage.

The work week went by without anything peculiar or especially taxing to do. On Wednesday evening when she would have joined Meg for dinner, Lindsay called and begged off. She instead went to her own Gray Gull. After a shower, a light meal and a cup of hot tea, Lindsay placed wood in the hearth and decided to just sit and enjoy the fire. She didn't want to read or paint – she just wanted to believe that she could exist. At nine that evening, there was a knock at her door and she answered it wearing pajamas and a robe. She was surprised to see Evan standing there.

"Is everything okay?" he asked. "Isn't this your usual night with Meg? I saw your car here on my way home and thought I'd check."

"I was tired. I felt like an evening here, I'm fine."

"Okay," he said slowly and then he looked into the main room of her home. "This looks very cozy," he said. "Any chance I could come in for a bit?"

Lindsay hesitated then stepped aside. "I suppose."

Evan walked in and looked at every detail, touching the mantle and seeming to like the room's arrangement.

He turned to look at her. "Is that tea you have there?"

Lindsay understood the hint. "Yes, would you like some?"

"I'd love it," he said as she walked to the tiny kitchen and poured another cup for him. When she walked back to the living room area, the only true room in the house, he sat down at one end of the sofa. She sat at the other end then noticed that she'd neglected to put slippers on her feet.

"This place holds such good memories for me. I loved Tilly. I was a terrible student with her form of art, but I really liked being in her company."

"What do you mean by her form of art? You're a very talented architect; I would have thought you'd be good with a paint brush."

Evan smiled. "Yeah, well I guess you'd call my style structured. Tilly did these ethereal little scenes – flowers without roots, crooked little houses by fairy-tale lakes. Her work looked like something from a child's story book, beautiful images. I haven't been able to get that loose about what I do. I like painting though – I like the use of color."

"Maybe you should consider painting as a way to relax. It's fun using paint to change the dynamics of something, and it doesn't matter what your style is – if your life is made happier for what you do, that's enough. Once when I was in my teens, I painted a blue pear." Lindsay smiled. "It had no message – I simply liked it, and one of my cousins liked it enough to hang it in his room. Painting saves me."

Evan looked at her then took a few swallows of tea.

"I know you've endured a lot losing your parents and your husband, but somehow, you've managed to come through all of that in one piece. I admire your stamina."

Lindsay said nothing – she was glad that he didn't know how fragmented she felt about the loneliness and displacement. She thought about how leaving Boston allowed her to at least rid her eyes of seeing all the familiar places she'd gone to with her family – now she had the issue of how to handle living in close proximity to Evan without him in her life.

The telephone rang and she looked at Evan as she stood to answer it. It was obvious by her expression that something was terribly wrong.

Evan walked to where she stood listening, almost whispering into the phone, "No, it can't be." When she placed the phone back on its receiver as if in a trance, Evan placed his hands on her arms.

"What is it, Lin? What's wrong?"

She dissolved into his arms and sobbed. When she could manage to speak she said, "It's Tess. She's dead."

Evan pulled her close and wrapped his arms around her as if he was trying to protect her from the truth. When she moved to sit down on the sofa, she covered her face with her hands and continued to cry. When she was able to stop, she explained that there had been an automobile accident – Tess had died at the scene.

"She always talked about how she didn't want to be thirty. She was twenty-nine. This can't have happened."

Evan sat down beside her and held her close for a long while. Near midnight he saw that she was asleep and he covered her with a warm blanket from her bedroom, then he sat down in a chair near to her and waited for daylight.

When she awoke in the morning, Lindsay saw Evan moving about in the galley kitchen and she could smell coffee. She thought about Tess. She was so beautiful, so vibrant, everyone loved her. Didn't all of that protect someone from death? She thought of a saying she recalled her grandmother using when it came to loss – *If love could have saved them, they would have lived forever.*

With two cups of coffee in his hands, Evan placed one on the low coffee table before her. He set his own cup near to hers then reached for her hands as she sat up, the blanket falling away from her shoulders.

"I'm so sorry, Lin. I'm so sorry."

Lindsay lived through the next few days as if in a trance. Along with relatives and friends of Tess, she mourned. Her funeral was the most difficult part. It was raining – Tess had hated the rain. It rained that fateful night of the accident.

As her glistening silver casket was lowered in to the ground, Lindsay could not resist watching it disappear beneath the earth. Tess would not want to be there. She loved bright colors and loud music. The depth of darkness and stillness was not for Tess. Somehow, somewhere in Lindsay's mind, her beautiful blonde friend had to live on.

Lindsay returned to work, but seeing Kathy and Deb only made the days seem impossible. Wherever they were, Tess had always been with them – Lindsay felt certain that they were feeling the same. When one of them mentioned Tess, the others would nod with tears flooding their eyes. At times, Lindsay would hear the clicking heels coming down the hallway – she would half expect to see Tess wearing those shoes.

The next few weeks brought cold November weather. The skies were often gray and threatened snow. Lindsay found the cold invigorating and began to think about Thanksgiving and Christmas. She'd learned to prepare good holiday meals with her Aunt Rose and wondered if Evan would consider inviting Meg and the Phillips family for some of the celebrations.

As she sat in the living room with a list and a pen, jotting down food she was thinking of preparing, Evan walked in from his room with blueprints in his hands.

He seemed surprised to see her there, making notes and drinking tea. "Hi," he said.

"Hi. Evan, could you spare me a few minutes?"

"Sure. What's up?" he said as he sat down across from her.

Lindsay sat up a little straighter. "I've been thinking about the holidays. How do you usually spend them?"

"For the past few years, I've had dinners at the base. However," he said with a smile, "I'm a married man now and open to suggestions."

"Who would have guessed?" Lindsay said.

"Guessed what?"

"That you could be agreeable."

Evan laughed. "I have my moments. So, what do you have in mind?"

"I was thinking of inviting Meg, Mary, Louisa, Joe, and Ricky Phillips, and Sara and Ben of course. I prepared holiday meals with my aunt over the years – I'm pretty efficient at it and I think it would be fun."

"Sounds great. But Sara and Ben have already made plans to go to her sister's place for a few days over each of the holidays. Let's tell them about it and go ahead and extend the invitations to the others. You do the planning – I can chop a mean onion – I'll assist."

"Okay," Lindsay said feeling light-hearted for the first time in a while.

Evan stood. "If that's all, I need to get back to this project. I have a deadline, a presentation first thing Monday morning."

Lindsay nodded. "I'll make the grocery list and I'll talk to you about it later. You might like specific food items that I'm not familiar with."

"Oh," he said with a smile as he walked away, "yes, like stuffed quahogs."

Thanksgiving morning, while Lindsay prepared vegetables and organized what she needed for stuffing, Sara walked into the kitchen. "I hope you have a wonderful holiday, Dear," she said.

Lindsay felt filled with joy until Sara picked up little Ginger. Adele looked up and Sara said, "My poor little mother. Don't you worry, Adele. Ginger will be treasured and thoroughly pampered. And when my sister comes here to visit, I shall insist that Ginger comes with her, and soon."

Lindsay felt a pain in her heart for the separation. She watched Adele as Sara left holding the kitten close. Charlie jumped on his mother, which seemed to pleasantly distract Adele enough that she boxed his little ears and then bathed him thoroughly. When Adele looked up, Lindsay talked to her about how well Ginger would do in her new home and she stroked her gently. Watching mother and son, Lindsay would keep her promise to get Charlie neutered, but somehow, she would persuade Evan to let Sara keep these two together. After all, what was one more cat?

Lindsay prepared a rich chestnut-apple dressing with plans to prepare whipped potato mixed with sour cream and chopped, sautéed scallions. There would be sweet potatoes cooked, sliced and lightly sautéed in maple syrup, green beans, butternut squash, cranberry sauce, and home made biscuits. Evan was in charge of the quahogs. For dessert, Lindsay planned for apple pie, chocolate brownies, and ice cream to go with either or both.

Evan walked into the kitchen around noon, with guests arriving at two.

"Whew!" he said. "This kitchen smells fantastic. You're making me starved. Anything I can do other than my quahogs?"

"Yes, as a matter of fact. I need those scallions chopped really fine. Other than that, I have things pretty much prepared. Oh, and you might select some wine to go with dinner – maybe a light and a dark?"

"Yes, Ma'am," he said with a smile.

"What's your favorite part of the meal?" she asked as she stirred sour cream into the whipped potato.

"Hmm," he said. "I guess the quahogs."

Lindsay stopped what she was doing, picked up an extra quahog shell and tossed it lightly at his back.

"Hey," he said as he approached her looking dangerous. He stopped less than an inch from her lips, as if he'd suddenly remembered that he was off course.

Lindsay breathed again as he backed away slowly and was glad when he set himself to work with a cutting board, scallions, and a sharp knife.

After the delicious meal had been served in the dining room, the table graced with forest green and white candles of varying shapes and sizes, Evan walked into the living room and set the prepared hearth to blaze. The men and Ricky ended up on the floor with a game of Monopoly while Meg, Louisa, and Lindsay talked about Christmas, their plans, and their purchases.

"It was good to be in this house again," Joe said as they were slipping their coats on and leaving. "I have great memories of the best peanut butter and jelly sandwiches in the world, made by Evan's mom, and playing around in the yard. We were never bored."

"I hope we'll have many more such times here," Evan said as he placed his hand lightly on Lindsay's shoulder, as if to include her in that package deal.

"I hope for more of these times too," Meg chirped in. "I've got a slice of apple pie and two brownies – Mary and I will have them when she gets home from her son's house tomorrow. Thank you both – this has been the nicest Thanksgiving I can recall in a very long time."

Lindsay sat down when everyone had gone, enjoying a glass of wine and the glowing hearth.

"You are one fantastic hostess," Evan said as he joined her. "My mom and Sara could cook, but that meal was the best I've ever had."

"Thank you," she said with a little smile. "I'm sure it was about your quahogs."

Evan laughed. "Did you like them?"

Lindsay couldn't help but smile – he seemed like a child showing off his latest drawing. "The quahogs were delicious. You may make them for me any time."

"I'd be glad to," he said with a serious note to his voice.

"So," she said, "we can do Christmas too?"

Evan sat back and crossed his right leg over his left knee. "I'm all for it. What kinds of traditions do you embrace? A tree, I'm sure."

"Oh, yes," Lindsay said. "A nice tree, although I'm prone to getting an artificial. They can stay up longer, like from now until New Year's, and it doesn't take the life from something young and growing."

"Okay," he said. "I'll put the ax back in my closet and we'll go get an artificial tree. I like them up early too – this weekend okay with you?"

"Yes," she said, "this weekend."

"So," he said, "this is probably a stupid question, but did you enjoy all of this? It was a lot of work for you."

Lindsay shifted in her seat and then stood. "I loved every bit of it. I enjoyed working in that magnificent kitchen with everything at my fingertips, and I loved the idea of preparing wonderful food for wonderful people."

"Does that include me?" he asked with a mischievous look on his face.

"Are you looking for compliments?" she asked. "Everything was wonderful, and that's all I'm going to say, except, I'm tired and going to bed. Goodnight, Evan."

As she walked out of the room and upstairs, she could only imagine how amazing it would feel to be holding his hand and taking him with her.

Chapter Fourteen

The Wednesday after Thanksgiving, Lindsay dined with Meg at her home. At that time, Meg revealed that she was thinking about another party, one to celebrate Christmas.

"Mike loved having parties," she said over coffee. "When we bought this place, it was good-naturedly referred to by the townsfolk as the dancehall. The original owners of the house made sure it had a ballroom. Mike used the room for racing around on his roller blades. It was really funny to see this salty old guy wearing nothing more than Hawaiian print bathing trunks skating around at fifty miles an hour. He loved it and, frankly, so did I. He had such a good time. I miss him terribly. However, he did love parties – I think he'd like to know that we were enjoying this place."

Lindsay smiled and took a sip of her coffee. "I wish I'd had the chance to know him. Aside from sounding intelligent and kind, he had the ability to have fun."

Meg closed her eyes for a moment and looked toward his portrait. "He sure did."

"I should probably go," Lindsay said as she finished her coffee. "I'm so tired these days. I think it's all about Tess – losing her has taken its toll on all of us at the office."

"I'm sure it has. It was a terrible tragedy and a huge adjustment."

Lindsay placed her cup down on the table next to her. "It will be nice to get home, maybe have a warm bath."

"Ah, you used the term home. You think of Evan's as home."

Lindsay stood and walked to where she'd left her coat. "Well, it's home for now."

"Don't you like him just a little?" Meg asked as she walked alongside Lindsay to the front door.

"Maybe," Lindsay said, "a little."

Meg laughed as she hugged Lindsay goodnight.

Lindsay drove home that night thinking about Meg's party. It would be good to hear laughter, music, and people all chattering at once. She also understood and accepted that being with Evan would be more painful than ever.

As she slipped into bed, she began to think about how she felt physically. She'd been tired, light-headed at times with a tinge of nausea for about a month. Lindsay jumped out of bed and reached for a small calendar in her purse. It confirmed what she suspected. She walked back to her bed and pulled the covers up to her chin, wondering what to do. Could she possibly stay in Cliff Point to raise her child? Should she go someplace new? It was unthinkable to raise his child elsewhere. In complete turmoil, she felt that Evan had regretted their night together and was now simply going through the necessary moves to help a friend. She couldn't tell him. At least not until the marriage was ended. The only reason she would fasten herself to a man was for love - not for his commitment to obligations. Within days, Lindsay saw an obstetrician who confirmed her pregnancy. This would be her secret for now – even from Meg.

With a party date set and the plans made, Lindsay began to think about what she would wear. She had a dress she loved and had worn often in Boston when going to the symphony or theater. It was cut just above the knee, a loose fitting black dress with sleeves to her wrists – simple yet striking.

On the day of the party, Lindsay sat in the kitchen, Adele and Charlie at her feet, drinking a cup of tea and browsing through a magazine. When Evan walked into the room, it startled her. Sara and Ben had gone off early; Lindsay had thought herself to be alone. Wearing a deep gray suit with a light green shirt and forest green tie, he looked like a fashion model.

"Good morning," he greeted her.

"Good morning," Lindsay said with her eyes back down to the magazine.

"What are you up to today?" he asked as he sat down across from her with a cup of coffee. I'm heading south for the day to see a client. Any interest in coming along?"

"South?"

"Boothbay."

"Oh," she said.

Evan smiled. "There's no sign of a storm. Are you afraid of getting stuck with me overnight again?"

Lindsay gave him a menacing look. "I'm not afraid of a storm and I'm not afraid of you either. Actually, if you can wait until I change clothes, I wouldn't mind going. I have Christmas shopping I'd like to do and I love Boothbay's shops."

"Sure, I'd be glad to wait until you change clothes – I think walking around in Boothbay with pajamas, robe, and fluffy slippers might just cause a bit of talk."

"Excuse me," she said as she stood and deposited her cup in the sink. "I'll just go slip into my red sequined ball gown and stiletto heels to match."

Evan smiled and sipped his coffee as she walked out of the room.

When they arrived in Boothbay, Evan left Lindsay in the center of town to shop while he went on to his appointment. She found hand knit sweaters for her Aunt Rose and family, a book on sailing ships for Ricky Phillips, a large rawhide bone for Sloop, and a stylish little brown hat with a peach colored peony rose fastened to its brim for Meg. She thought about what to get Sara, Ben, and Evan, but there was still time.

As she walked around a corner with her arms filled with purchases, she collided with another human being and the packages spilled over a six-foot length of sidewalk. Lindsay looked up startled and met Evan's blue eyes.

"Have we met somewhere before? Maybe the library?" he said with a smile.

Lindsay sighed - the man was a menace.

"Do you want to get back now?" she asked.

"I guess we could, but if you have more shopping to do, I wouldn't mind doing a little myself."

"I'd love another hour," Lindsay said. "Then maybe we could grab a coffee to head back with."

"Okay," he said. "My car is just across the street – let's get rid of these packages and my briefcase. We'll have coffee and a bite to eat first, then we'll have the energy to shop. You look a little worn."

"Great. Thanks – it's lovely looking worn."

Evan laughed. "You look worn in a good way."

"Seriously?"

Evan laughed again as he placed the packages in the trunk of his car.

Over lunch he asked, "So, other than Sara and Ben, who do you need to shop for?"

"I'd like to pick up little gifts for Kathy, Deb, and Mrs. Sinnott. I'd like to find something in the way of a toy or a book for little Audra. Oh, and I need gifts for Adele and Charlie."

Evan raised his eyebrows. "What about me?"

"What about you?"

"Aren't you planning to buy me anything?"

Lindsay wanted to laugh, but she kept a serious look on her face. "Oh. I suppose I might."

She was certain that Evan was frowning, but since she didn't look at him for fear of laughing out loud, she looked away and forced her eyes to focus on the busy sidewalks of beautiful Boothbay Harbor.

When they left the restaurant and walked, enjoying the windows decorated for Christmas, Lindsay caught sight of an enchanting music box. It was made to look like a carousel, with hand carved wooden figures, children on ponies circling and dancing with the melody. "Look," she said, "isn't that the most wonderful music box you've ever seen?"

Evan put his face close to the window to eliminate glare from the emerging sun. "Yes, that's nice, but I think we should get on with our shopping."

Lindsay's heart sank. She wanted to buy that music box for her baby. Evan seemed in a hurry; she crossed the street with him and continued to shop.

Before driving back to Cliff Point, Evan suggested coffee in a little café overlooking the harbor. "So," he said, "are you pleased with your purchases?"

"Yes, I think so. The assortment of teas and jellies for Sara and Ben makes a practical gift, yet fun. And I have two really good catnip mice for Adele and Charlie. I picked up an extra for Sara to take to Ginger at her sister's house."

Evan looked across the table to her pale blue eyes and said, "Tell me how you judge a good catnip mouse."

Lindsay looked from the harbor to his face. "By the strength of smell - they have to be very aromatic."

Evan's lips started to form a smile but then he seemed to restrain himself. "Oh, and then do you roll around on a rug with it?"

Lindsay scowled at him and said nothing in reply.

"Are we ready to go?" he asked as he drained the last of his coffee into his appealing mouth.

"Yes, I'm ready to finish shopping and go home. We need to get ready for Meg's party tonight too."

"You referred to Cliff Point as home. Do you really feel that way?"

"I love it there. I've left my past behind – Cliff Point means everything to me. It would take something huge to make me leave."

Their drive home was uneventful and quiet. Lindsay was tired and allowed her head to rest back against the seat. Evan looked over at her a few times, but did not engage her in conversation. She looked like she needed a little nap. At home, she showered and changed, organized her purchases, then slipped into her black dress and strappy black heels. She was not yet showing any signs of her pregnancy – her profile was still of a slim young woman. She took a deep breath then walked downstairs to see Evan waiting in the hallway. His eyes seemed to appraise her as if he was considering buying. With his hands tucked into dark brown slacks, his cocoa colored sports coat looked perfect with his white shirt open at the throat. Lindsay looked at him and thought that she would very much enjoy kissing that throat, and more.

"You look nice," he said when she took her last stair tread and was standing a few feet away from him.

"Thank you. You look nice too. I was thinking, should we take something to Meg's? Maybe stop for some wine or something?"

"I took care of it," he said. "I had the florist in town send her a bouquet of red roses and holly, and I have a nice bottle of brandy in the car she may enjoy with a smaller guest list at some point."

"You think of everything," she said as he helped her into her long coat.

During the five minute car ride, Evan asked about Christmas which was only ten days away.

"Did you make any plans for the holiday yet? You had mentioned inviting the Phillips family and Meg. Did that change?"

"I mentioned it to Louisa. They wouldn't mind getting together with us at some time, but on Christmas Day they're going over to New Hampshire to Louisa's parents. I mentioned it to Meg and she's up for Christmas Eve or Christmas Day. Mary is going someplace Christmas Eve, so I was wondering if we should do something to gather and celebrate on Christmas Eve. I could do a buffet. That way, Meg and Mary could be together for Christmas, and I guess that leaves you and me together for the day itself. It gets confusing – everyone is going in different directions. What do you think?"

Evan smiled in the darkness of the car; Lindsay saw the flexing of his jaw with on-coming car lights and knew he was amused.

"Maybe you'd prefer to do something else," she said.

"I have no plans. I think it would be just fine to spend time with our friends on Christmas Eve. On Christmas, you and I could enjoy a quiet day. We'll have Adele and Charlie – we can practice being parents with them – you know, teach them table manners and stuff."

Lindsay looked out to the dark just before they pulled in to Meg's driveway and parked. She appreciated Evan's attempt at humor, but between his remark about practicing to be parents and the fact that this time of year evoked a sadness in thinking of her mother and father, her capacity for humor was small. How excited they would be to know that a baby was on its way. They had both loved Christmas – learning of a grandchild would have made the most perfect of gifts.

"Would you like to mention Christmas Eve to Louisa, Joe, and Meg? We could start the evening at seven."

"Sure," Evan said, "I'll talk to them. We'll have to get the house decorated. How about if we go tomorrow to pick up a tree – your artificial tree? There are tons of ornaments in the attic – unless you'd rather have new ones."

"I'd like to use the old ones, and maybe add a new one for this year."

"Okay. It's a date. Tomorrow we buy a tree and put it up. You're in charge of making hot cocoa though."

"Why me?" she asked.

"Because I don't know how to make real cocoa - I want real cocoa."

Lindsay frowned. She didn't know how to make real cocoa either – she was familiar with the packaged mix and hot water.

"Do you have real cocoa in the house?"

"We always have it – my mother insisted and Sara kept up the tradition."

Lindsay started to open the door to the car when Evan walked around to her side and opened it for her, extending his warm hand to her. She enjoyed his good manners and she would figure out how to make real cocoa.

"Ready?" he said.

Chapter Fifteen

Meg's house was alive with Christmas - red candles flickered like little living spirits and Evan's gift of red roses met them on the entranceway table, across from closets where guests left their coats. Christmas carols could be heard coming from Meg's ballroom and the scent of burning maple and balsam filled the air from the blazing hearth in the parlor. She had planned this event well. Lindsay felt sad for her that she must certainly be remembering holidays with her beloved Mike.

Meg appeared in a floor-length white dress, looking like a snow queen. "My favorite people," she whispered to Lindsay and Evan. "You two look gorgeous together. Go and find your table – I'm sitting with you. There are about forty people coming tonight – five tables, eight at each. We're going to have a darn good time!"

Evan gently nudged Lindsay toward the ballroom with his hand at her back. There, they found their table, name cards at each chair, small bouquets of red poinsettias and holly at the center of each white cloth. With low lighting and candles on each table, the room looked naturally festive without being overdone.

As they sat down, Evan's friend from the base, Tom Whitcomb, greeted them. "Evan," he began, his eyes moving from Evan to Lindsay then back to Evan, "you're a lucky man."

"I did notice," Evan said as he shook hands with Tom and gave Lindsay just a trace of a smile.

"If he'll part with you," Tom said with a wink to Lindsay, "save me a dance," and then he was gone.

Before they could say more, Louisa and Joe Phillips joined their table, and then Mary, Ted McNee and Keith Hatherly. Evan looked up in complete surprise at seeing Keith. He stood and hugged his friend then asked how he was and when had he been discharged from the hospital.

"Today," Keith said. "When Meg invited me here as kind of a

surprise for you, I was more than thrilled. It's good to be out and about, even on crutches. Ted gave me a ride, I can't drive quite yet. But," he said looking at Lindsay and then Evan again, "I don't know how to thank the two of you. You've saved Sean and me."

"Are you out of the hospital for good?" Evan asked.

Lindsay's heart felt like it might stop. *Was this the end of the road?*

"I'm in transition. I'll be staying at the guest house where Sean and I can spend more time together; I'll have physical therapy every day, but I won't need to stay in a bed – in fact, I've been encouraged to move around as long as the pain is minimal. I feel great – I'm on my way back to being my old self."

"Lindsay," Keith began, "I felt sorry for Evan having to do this wedding stint for me, but meeting you, I know he's been just fine. She's a keeper," he said to Evan.

Evan smiled and nodded, not looking at Lindsay at all.

Again, although Lindsay smiled when speaking with Keith, she felt a tremendous lump in her throat for the future which might suddenly be changed. Could she count on Christmas with Evan? After tonight, would everything be over? The delicious meal was served and Lindsay noted that Evan's appetite was not his usual – hers was nonexistent. She noticed too that he seemed to be having more wine than normal – she avoided the alcohol and decided that she would insist on driving home. Accidents had taken her parents, Peter, and Tess. No more.

"May I have this dance?" Ted McNee extended his hand to Lindsay and she accepted.

At one point from the dance floor, she allowed her eyes to go back to her table, to Evan, but he was not there. When the dance was over, she thanked Ted and sat down, glad for the chance to take a few sips of water. Her eyes scanned the room for Evan – he was no where in sight.

"Where's your other half?" Louisa asked. "Joe and I got up to dance – when we came back, he was gone."

"I don't know," Lindsay said. "He may be helping Meg with something."

Louisa slid closer to Lindsay. "Is everything okay? I mean, you know you don't have to explain anything to me – I know your little secret, but when we were together at Thanksgiving, you and Evan seemed so in sync. I was hoping you two would really lock into one another."

Lindsay took a sip of water. "It kind of goes back and forth, Louisa. I think he starts to warm up to me, then he backs off. Maybe I do the same. I don't know. It's such a strange predicament we found ourselves in. I'm glad we did it – especially seeing Keith looking so happy and well tonight, but it's pretty awkward sometimes."

Louisa nodded. "I can imagine."

Evan came back to the table with two fresh drinks just as Joe reached for Louisa's hand. "We don't get out much to go dancing," he said. "Let's go out there and show'em how to do the twist."

Louisa rolled her eyes and smiled at Lindsay. Before she could take her thoughts back to Evan, Ted McNee came along again and invited Lindsay to dance. By the time he coaxed her out to the dance floor, the twist was gone and a slow dance evolved. Ted held Lindsay respectably close, enough so that they could talk.

"Are you two doing all right? I haven't seen you on the dance floor with your husband all night."

Lindsay tried to smile. "I think we're both tired. We went to Boothbay today. Evan met with a client and then we Christmas shopped. It's been a long day - a very nice day but still tiring."

Ted didn't ask any more questions. When he returned her to the table where Evan sat, he gave his friend some advice. "If you don't get this beautiful woman out on the dance floor, I'm coming back for her." He smiled at Lindsay and winked at Evan then left to talk to a friend at the bar.

"Are you having a good time?" Evan asked after several moments of silence.

"Yes, it's a beautiful party."

"How much longer would you like to stay? It's nearly eleven."

"Oh," she said, "I didn't know it was that late. Did you want to go?"

"Go where?" Meg asked as she came around the corner. "You two haven't had a single dance. I think you should."

Evan looked at Lindsay. "Shall we?"

"If you want to, but really, we don't have to pretend any more."

Evan looked stunned.

Meg looked from one to the other. "Listen," she said, "Keith is doing great, but the last thing you want to do is anger the social worker and the courts. Let's see this thing through until Keith is completely healed. He's not capable of looking after a little boy yet. Now go out on that dance floor – don't pretend to be happy – be happy."

Evan hesitated but then he stood and took Lindsay's hand, leading her out to dance to a slow song. At first he held her as he might a friend, then he held her as a lover holds a lover. Lindsay closed her eyes and allowed him to move her slowly through the romantic music. At times she could feel a gentle pressure on her right hand, a tightening of his grasp to her back. She wanted everything to be genuine – but was it? How wonderful it would be to shout out to the guests that a baby was on its way – or how tragic might that announcement be? It all depended on Evan.

When the music stopped, they found themselves beneath one of many sprigs of mistletoe. Evan looked around the room, his eyes seeing other couples kissing. Lindsay saw what he did, and then she felt his lips on hers - for the sake of appearing to be a couple in love – or for love? She didn't know how Evan felt – her own emotions were high.

They walked toward their table with the intention of saying goodnight. About half of the guests had left, Louisa and Joe included. They'd left Ricky at the home of another friend – they wanted to pick him up before the night grew later. As Lindsay bent to retrieve her purse, she nearly fell forward. Evan caught her by the shoulders, but not before both Meg and Ted noticed.

"Lindsay, are you all right, Dear?" Meg asked.

Ted had a look of concern on his face. "Did you trip on something? Really, Lindsay, are you okay?"

Evan held her firmly by her shoulders, then slipped one arm around her waist.

"I'm fine – just a little fuzzy. I did a lot of shopping today, and although I've had a wonderful evening dancing, I think I'm just in need of my warm bed."

If anyone noticed, they didn't say anything about her use of *my* instead of *our* warm bed.

Evan looked at his watch. "I'm taking you home." His words were firm, matter-of-fact. No one begged them to stay. Evan urged Lindsay to sit down while he fetched his and her coats from the front closet. "Let's go," he said as he took her arm and helped her to her feet.

"I'm okay," she said to Meg's worried face. "Really, I loved the party. Everything was wonderful. Thank you," she said as she leaned forward to deliver a hug. "And Ted, it was very nice dancing with you," she said with a smile.

"It was my pleasure," he said as he gently squeezed her hand.

"All set?" Evan asked.

When Lindsay indicated that she was, Evan thanked Meg and said goodnight as he led Lindsay to his car. Inside his home, he took her coat and hung it in the closet then urged her to let him help her upstairs. "Do you want anything to eat or drink before you go up?"

"No, but I was going to check on Adele and Charlie."

"I'll take care of them. Right now, you're going to bed. And if you don't feel better tomorrow, I'm going to insist that you see a doctor."

"We're getting our tree tomorrow."

"We're getting our tree if you're okay."

When they reached Lindsay's room, Evan walked in with her. The room was warm but he asked if she'd like a fire.

"Not tonight," she said. "I'll be asleep before I can enjoy it. Thank you, Evan. I'm sorry I worried everyone tonight. I'm just tired."

"Do you need help unzipping that dress?"

Lindsay sat down on her bed and kicked off her shoes. "No, thank you – there's no zipper. It's a stretchy fabric, it just goes over my head."

"And you can manage that on your own? I don't want you hanging yourself or anything."

Lindsay laughed. "Not to worry," she said. "Goodnight, Evan."

He didn't say goodnight. He looked at her as if she might melt, then he turned and left her room, closing the door behind him.

Lindsay pulled a nightgown from a drawer and slipped out of her dress and underclothes. The nightgown went over her head as had the dress and, without further fussing with clothing she pulled the covers down and climbed into bed. She was definitely tired, but she'd had a wonderful day. Shopping in Boothbay with Evan, the party with people she cared for at Meg's – it was all time filled with joy. She went to sleep feeling very grateful.

At three in the morning, she woke up and was thirsty. She thought about what to do – there were no glasses to fill with water upstairs – she would need to go down to the kitchen. She stepped into slippers and, without a robe, took her chances that she would not see Evan. In the kitchen, she found a very sleepy Adele curled up in a rocking chair with Charlie. Quietly, she ran a glass of cold water for herself and checked to see that the cats were all set. They were – Evan had filled their food and water bowls. Up in her room she went back to her bed and thought about the baby. Boy or girl? What would she name this child? Wouldn't she love to have input on that from his father? Thinking of this new little life to love, she went back to sleep.

Chapter Sixteen

In the morning, Lindsay woke early and dressed. She felt rested and energized by thoughts of going to shop for a Christmas tree. In the kitchen, she fed the cats then placed the kettle on for tea. Coffee wasn't agreeing with her quite as well with her little passenger, although she missed its taste.

"Good morning," Evan said as he walked into the kitchen and saw Lindsay sitting at the table with an English muffin and tea - a small local newspaper spread before her. "How are you this morning?"

Lindsay looked up at him. "I'm fine. We're going to get the tree, right?"

Evan laughed. "Determined, aren't you?"

"Yes. You promised. I'm fine – I feel great. We need the tree."

Evan poured himself some tea and then looked at it. "How come we're having tea these days? Why the switch?"

"I just like tea sometimes. If you want coffee, I can make some in the French press – it will only take a few minutes."

"No," he said, "I'll do with the tea for now. We'll make coffee later. So, the tree - McLaren's in town has artificial trees – that's what you want, right?"

"Right."

"Okay. So, do you want to go with me, or do you want to tell me how large you want this tree to be. I think they go to eight feet, and a variety of heights below that. Where are you thinking of placing it?"

Lindsay looked outside through a French door, then back at Evan. "Where did your Christmas tree go when you were a child?"

"To the right of the hearth in the living room."

"I like that idea. We can enjoy looking at the tree and the hearth at the same time. I was also wondering if we could have another tree. Maybe a six-foot one in the living room and a two-foot one in the kitchen. Those are the two rooms where we spend the most time. It would be cheerful to have little lights and pretty decorations in both places."

Evan finished his tea and left the cup by the sink. "Sounds reasonable. Now, do you want to come with me, or should I just go get the trees?"

"If you don't mind, I'll stay here. I'll even make coffee while you're gone."

"Deal," he said. "I should be back within an hour."

"And then we'll put the trees up?"

"When I get back I have about one hour's worth of finishing touches to some plans I'm working on for the library – one hour, I promise, and then we'll put up the trees."

"Okay. That's fine. And with Sara and Ben away for the weekend, one of us needs to plan for food. We have all sorts of stuff in the freezer. Do you have a particular craving?"

"No, do you?"

Lindsay gulped – had he noticed her slightly enlarged area of abdomen? "No, not unless you're up to a pizza later. I've been thinking about pizza."

"Pizza sounds good. I can go down town for that later. Right now, I'm off to get the trees and some new lights. White or colored?"

"A few sets of tiny white lights for the living room tree, and maybe a set of colored to mix with a set of white for the little kitchen tree. How about that?"

Evan stood with his hands on his hips. "I like that idea. Now, you're making cookies and we'll sing carols while we decorate, right?"

"Absolutely," she said.

When he walked out of the kitchen to head for his car, Lindsay thought about the cookies. She went into the pantry and found what she wanted, almonds and almond flavoring. Good. She would make Angel Stars with sprinkles of white sugar on the top: one of her mother's favorite recipes. She assembled the ingredients on the table, found the perfect large mixing bowl, and felt a sense of happiness mingled with sadness. Becoming a parent, Lindsay was at a heightened state of mind thinking of how her own mother must have felt when she was expecting a child. She hoped that somehow her parents knew. And although the Angel Star cookies were for Evan while decorating the tree with celebration, they would also be for her parents – her mother who loved baking them and her father who loved eating them.

When Evan returned, he walked into the kitchen and announced that he had everything set for the launching of their trees. He would see her in one hour.

"What's all this?" he asked as he noticed the assembled ingredients.

"You said you wanted cookies – you'll have cookies. I hope you like almond flavoring. If you don't, I'll make some other kind."

"Almond is my favorite," he said. "My birthday cake every year after I was nine or ten was covered with a white almond frosting, and there might even have been some almond flavoring in the cake – anyway, I love almond. How did you know?"

Lindsay smiled. "My secret."

He gave her a quizzical look then walked toward his workroom. Lindsay thought about the secret – it was about so much more than cookies.

During the next twenty minutes, she began to mix her dry ingredients. She added the eggs, melted butter, and flavoring. The oven was set to three-hundred and fifty degrees and within a short time the delectable aroma began to fill the kitchen. Before his hour was up, Evan peeked in to see if any of the cookies were ready. The first batch of twelve was cooling on a rack. "I can't stand it," he said. "I need to steal one of these right now." He hesitated and looked at her face as she cut a new batch into three-inch stars. "May I?"

Lindsay smiled. "Of course. Is your hour up already?"

"No – give me another twenty minutes and I'm at your service. Oh," he said after one bite of a star, "these things are great. Thanks." And he was gone.

Lindsay continued to bake until there were four dozen sparkling stars. She left several on a plate for Evan to help himself, then placed the remaining cookies in a large tin to keep them fresh. It had been at least fourteen years since she'd last made these sweets with her mother, Caroline Heddon.

When his hour was up, exactly on time as he'd promised, Evan walked toward the hallway on his way to find Lindsay. She was already there, her hands behind her back, ready to get started.

"Living room or kitchen first?" he asked.

"I think it would be nice to decorate the living room first, then while we have pizza later, we can do the little kitchen tree."

"Okay, great idea," he said as he took the large artificial tree out of its box. "I think we should buy some real greens. You know, balsam and holly to put on the mantles and such. It will smell good too."

"We could also buy garlands of laurel or boxwood for the mantle and the archway between the living room and hall. And we'll need a wreath for the front door. I have some really nice bright red ribbon – I could make a beautiful bow if you buy a plain wreath."

"The red bow sounds good. Maybe a boxwood wreath would be nice too. I'll see what I can find when I go out for the pizza later. A couple of different places have greens for sale." With another cookie and a cup of coffee at his disposal, Evan began to straighten branches and adjust the stand. The lights went on first and were moved about as needed. The tree was then maneuvered to the corner, moving a chair to the right just a bit to accommodate the enchanting sight. Evan and Lindsay stood back admiring the shape and glow – it was beautiful.

"Do you like it?" he asked as he turned to look at her glowing, pretty face.

"I love it," she said as her eyes watered and stayed fastened to the tree's shimmering lights. Without thinking, she placed her right hand on her abdomen, then realizing what she'd done, she quickly moved it and asked about the trunk filled with decorations.

"Yup, I need to go up to the attic. I'll just be a minute. You could grab me another one of those cookies while I'm gone – all this takes energy you know."

Lindsay hesitated as he left, patted her eyes dry and then went to the kitchen for more coffee and cookies for Evan – tea for her.

Their entire day was happily taken with decorating the trees. Some unnecessary help was offered from Adele and Charlie in the kitchen. When Evan went out for pizza at three, he came back with ropes of garland, two different wreathes, and bundles of balsam and holly. "We," he said as he left them in the entrance way from outside to the kitchen, "are going to be the most festive house in town."

"It's all going to be perfect. Have I dragged you away from your work to do something you might have passed up?"

"Are you kidding?" he asked. "I love this. I haven't done anything like this in years. My mother decorated everything. My father used to say that he had to watch it; if he sat still too long around the holidays, she'd decorate him."

Lindsay laughed. She wished she'd known Amanda and Douglas

Drury.

"So you were friends with Joe Phillips as a boy, but was there anyone else?"

"A couple of people. One of them moved away pretty young, in his early teens, down south someplace. The other fellow, Jeb, moved to Seattle. He went to college out that way, met a girl from there and stayed. Cliff Point is a small town. I pretty much knew everyone. What about you? Boston must have been huge compared to what I experienced in a small town and private school."

"I guess so," Lindsay said. "It didn't occur to me that anyone did anything different. When the accident happened, I went to live in a country type of town. I was new to being a teen – it was not the easiest of transitions. I really missed our house in Cambridge too. Everything changed. I suppose that's the way it is – we're all vulnerable to what happens next."

Evan looked at her and seemed to sense her sadness. At that moment, a grandfather clock in the hallway chimed and Lindsay looked in its direction. "Clocks," she said, "they're like living things. When I was little, I used to think that the ticking of a clock was its heart beat. I don't know how anyone could throw a clock away – at least one that works."

"You know," he teased, "it's probably not wise to get caught up with caring about an inanimate object."

"What, you never loved a teddy bear?"

"Oh, yeah," he said. "I still sleep with mine every night."

Lindsay looked at him and he laughed. He helped himself to another slice of pizza and then asked, "What's next? We've decorated the trees; how about if we get a fire going in the living room hearth and then fool around putting up the garland and other stuff. Sara and Ben are going to be amazed when they come home tomorrow."

"I think they'll enjoy it all. Sara spends her days between their rooms and the kitchen – they'll like the little tree."

"They will. You know, I wonder sometimes if they stay here because of me. They go to Sara's sister's house often – I keep waiting for them to tell me they're moving there. She has a large house in Damariscotta, toward Pemaquid Point. They like it there."

"Pemaquid Point? I think I've heard of it, but I haven't been there."

"Really? It's gorgeous. It's a peninsula where a lighthouse stands at the crest of outstanding rock formations. I could sit there all day and watch the waves' endless thrashing against the massive cliffs. We should go there someday – maybe in the spring."

Lindsay thought about spring – from the doctor's calculations, this baby would be coming into this world in late June.

"I'd love to go there," Lindsay said.

Evan looked at her as he held his coffee mug in both hands. "Then we will."

Chapter Seventeen

The next several days brought skies dotted with wispy snowflakes. There was nothing in the way of a threatening storm - just the routine of work during the day and evenings by a mellow fire.

That Evan's workroom was just off the living room inspired Lindsay to spend leisure time there reading - wrapping time was spent in the kitchen. She had managed to find gifts for everyone on her list except Evan. In her quest to find him the perfect gift, she found little objects to place around the house: tea-light candles, red and white candy canes, and two little figures of deer.

When he walked into the living room on his way to the kitchen for coffee, he found Lindsay sitting by the tree and fire, a book in her hands. "William Faulkner?" he asked as he stopped for a moment.

"No, I finished that one. This is Michener. I read it years ago, but I decided to read it again."

Evan nodded. "I'm getting some coffee – can I bring you anything?"

"Thank you, I'm all set – tea." She held up a half-full cup.

When he had filled his cup with coffee and went back toward the living room Lindsay noticed he had a rock in his hand.

"Why the rock?" she asked.

"Oh, my blueprints keep sliding toward the bottom of my slanted table – I don't like to use tape to hold the top in place – thought a rock would help."

Lindsay thought that was a clever idea, but maybe something she had in her possession would make a perfect Christmas gift for him. She went upstairs and looked through a carton in her closet - a few items that had once belonged to her parents. Yes, this would work, this and one other item.

Back downstairs, she found Evan poking at the fire. "There you are. I thought maybe you'd gone to bed early. I was a little worried."

"I'm fine," she said as she sat down and picked up her tea cup.

"It's after nine – I'm done for the night. Can I offer you a nightcap? I was thinking of having a little brandy."

"No, thanks," she answered quickly. There would be no alcohol for her while carrying this child. "Maybe some other time."

Evan poured himself a small measure of the amber colored drink then sat down with his feet up on an ottoman. "This is nice."

"A cozy fire is always in order," she said as she dreamily watched the flickering flames.

"It's not just the fire. It's the tree, it's the laurel garland, it's us in this old house making it breathe again."

Lindsay looked at him, not sure what he meant.

"I'll be sorry to see it end in some ways," he said.

That statement pierced her heart. She said nothing.

"Are you sure you're okay with having the Christmas Eve buffet? That's a lot of work, and you've seemed a little tired lately. You've had a lot to deal with between losing your friend at work and dealing with this façade."

Again, *façade*; the word was powerful. How had she allowed herself to become so immersed in this man when it seemed he was thinking about it being over?

"I'll enjoy doing the buffet. I'm not the greatest cook in the world, but I know how to prepare a few things that should be tasty."

"How can I help?"

Lindsay looked from the fire to his eyes. "Would you like to make your stuffed quahogs again? Everyone enjoyed them at Thanksgiving."

"Okay. And I make a mean salad. I'll do quahogs and salad."

Christmas Eve felt magical, filling the house with friends and good food. Lindsay loved entertaining and Evan seemed to enjoy every aspect of the night. When everyone had gone home, Evan complimented Lindsay on her preparations and helped her to clear the dishes and stemware – together they worked until the kitchen had no remnants of the night.

"So," he said as they finished the last of their cleanup, "are you waiting up for Santa?"

Lindsay smiled. "Maybe. What about you?"

"Well, we have gifts under the tree from Meg and the Phillips – do you want to open them now or wait until morning?"

"What did you do as a child?"

Evan looked at her for a long while before he said, "You know Lindsay, I would give anything to get my folks back, and I know you feel the same. And I think it's nice to have some of their traditions, but I also hope that we can develop some of our own. You know, like the tree in the kitchen. I almost love that tree more than the big one – it's ours."

Lindsay was quiet; she could not help thinking about what Christmas next year and the years after that would bring. Surely it would not be the same – not in this house. There would be a child and toys – but there would be no Evan.

She looked at him. "You're right. We need to learn to move on."

"So, again I ask – gifts tonight or gifts tomorrow? Let's not consider what was done when we were younger – let's do what we want to do."

"Okay," she said. "Let's open our gifts tonight. And then in the morning, we can fix ourselves a massive breakfast and then go for a walk. We could walk to Meg's. I have something I forgot to give her with her gift."

After opening their gifts from Meg and the Phillips, Evan placed a large package in Lindsay's lap. She told him that the two packages in white with the red bows were for him. When he untied the ribbon and tore the paper gently from the first package, he found a framed painting – the one she had begun in Bermuda. Evan seemed stunned as he looked at it over and over. Then his eyes met hers.

"This is amazing and unexpected."

"You mentioned wanting one of my paintings for over your workroom's mantle the day you gave Meg and me a tour. I hope you'll enjoy it." She wanted to add that the aqua color of the sea in that scene was the very color of his eyes – but she did not.

Evan placed the painting gently against a chair and looked at it from eight feet away. "It's perfect," he said.

"Open the little package," Lindsay said.

"What about your gift from me – don't you want to open that?"

She looked down at the beautifully wrapped package. "Yes, but open the little present first."

Evan opened the gift and took from the box a beautiful cobalt blue paper weight. He looked at Lindsay and she thought he looked speechless. "To replace the rock," he said.

"Yes, to replace the rock. It was a prized possession of my father. It had been his father's before him. I haven't had many of my parents' favorite things around me for a long time, but I think it's appropriate now to give new life to these objects once treasured. I hope you'll enjoy using it."

Evan looked as though he was going to get up and take her in his arms, and she wanted him to, but instead he said, "I love it, Lindsay. I'll take good care of it. Now how about if you open your gift from me."

Lindsay untied the ravishing bow in shades of green and gold against a luminous gold paper. This item, whatever it was, had been professionally wrapped, no doubt about that. She was careful, hoping to preserve as much of the paper and ribbon as possible. When she reached the inside, the top of the box lifted off to reveal billowy white and gold tissue paper. She pulled the layers away and then covered her mouth as she gasped. The beautiful carousel music box was there, waiting to be heard. The traitorous tears fell.

Evan moved and sat down on the sofa next to where she sat. He lifted the music box from its container and moved the carton to the floor. He looked at her tears.

"Lindsay, I didn't mean to make you cry. I thought you'd like this – I saw the look in your eyes that day in Boothbay when you watched these little figures move."

Lindsay wiped her eyes and took a deep breath. She nodded.

Evan put a hand on her shoulder. "Are you all right?"

Lindsay felt very confused. She wanted him to embrace her, but not in this situation, not unless it was for the right reason. She was determined to regain her composure.

"I'm fine," she said. "It's just that this is such a special gift, Evan. Thank you. You're right, I was mesmerized when I saw it in Boothbay – it's absolutely wonderful."

"This," he said, "is all terrific. We found great gifts for one another and this evening with friends was the best. I'll never forget anything about tonight."

Lindsay felt almost weak with emotion. She reached for the music box and Evan lifted it to her lap. She pulled a small knob on its side and watched as the little ponies went round and round to an old-fashioned tune. They watched and listened for a few minutes and then Lindsay pushed the knob in and everything stopped. How simple she thought it would be if all of life could be controlled that easily.

"Shall we give Adele and Charlie their catnip mice?" Evan asked.

"Maybe we should see if they're awake. If not, we could wait until morning."

Together they tip-toed to the kitchen where they found that Adele and Charlie had made themselves comfortable on a little rug beneath the tiny tree. Both of them fast asleep, Evan and Lindsay looked at one another.

"Can you imagine if we had kids? Here we are, sneaking around two cats like they might be waiting for what, Cat-me-claus?"

Lindsay smiled. "I think we should wait until morning," she whispered, "the catnip will get them all wound up and they're so sleepy looking."

Evan nodded. "Okay, the kids wait until morning."

They left the kitchen quietly, turning down the light, then walked to the front hall.

"I think I'm going up," Lindsay said. "But thank you again for the wonderful carousel. It's charming." She so wanted to tell him how their child would love listening to the gentle music as it lulled him or her to sleep.

"I'm glad you like it," Evan said. "The picture and the paperweight are incredible, Lindsay. I'm overwhelmed with your thoughtfulness."

They looked at one another for a moment, neither of them making a move to embrace. Lindsay turned and walked up the stairs to her room. Inside, she leaned against the door for a moment and then she changed to night clothes and made herself comfortable in bed.

Christmas morning brought a gift of its own – a combination of snowflakes and sunshine, creating a shower of gold.

Dressed in jeans and a thick coffee colored sweater, Lindsay went downstairs to the kitchen. There she was surprised to find Evan at the center table mixing something in a large bowl. He looked up at her and smiled. "Merry Christmas," he said.

"Merry Christmas," she returned. She glanced quickly down at Adele and Charlie who were eating happily from their bowl. "What do they have?" she asked. "They seem to be ravenous."

"I gave them some left over chicken as their Christmas treat. They found their presents before I came down – I guess those catnip mice you chose are pretty aromatic."

Lindsay smiled at the cats' enthusiasm for their breakfast.

"What are you making over there?" she asked peeking into the bowl.

"Pancakes. I'm following an old recipe – I don't know where it came from, my mother or Sara. I've had them, not made by me, but they've been good. We also have some fruit – I cut up some apples and we have grapes. What else would you like? I'm sure we have turkey bacon; Sara and Ben live on it. Any suggestions?"

Lindsay smiled at his efforts. "I'm fine with the pancakes and fruit. I see you've made coffee in the French press – I think I'll make myself a cup of tea."

"Did you notice how pretty it is out there today?" he asked. "It's like one of those scenes from a movie or something."

"I noticed," Lindsay said. "I think it's very fitting for such a special day."

Evan stopped mixing and turned the fire low under a griddle on the stove. He looked at her and then took a sip of coffee. "We'll give the griddle warm up time," he said. "And while we have a few minutes, I'd like to ask you about today. I know you want to walk to Meg's with something you forgot to give her last night, but is there anything else you'd like to do? I mean, it's Christmas. Will you call your aunt? Or is there something else we can do to make this day merrier for you?"

Lindsay ate a few grapes as she went about making her tea. She told Evan that she thought the griddle was now warm enough and then she said, "Yes, I'll telephone Aunt Rose later. The mornings are busy for her – I have four cousins who are all married, three of them with children. Aunt Rose will be in the middle of food preparation just now. As for the rest of the day, we have lots of leftovers from last night, and I have no expectations. I look forward to a walk, seeing Meg briefly, and coming back here will be nice. I might like a quick visit to my cottage – I feel that I cheated it out of Christmas this year."

Evan smiled as he spooned small pancakes onto the griddle. "Okay – are you going to tell me what it is you have for Meg or is it a secret?"

Lindsay moved to the pantry and two tins. She opened one of them to reveal more of her almond Angel Stars. "These are for you," she said, "and this tin is for Meg and Mary to enjoy. No secret." And then she felt guilty because there definitely was a secret.

"Hey," he said, "that was very thoughtful of you. Thank you. I love these things."

After enjoying a pancake and fruit breakfast, and then each of them relaxing in the living room by the fire with coffee and tea, Lindsay asked if Evan was up for that walk.

He looked at his watch then at her. "Sure, it's almost noon, sounds like a good time to go. The sun has skipped away, but it's still nice out. Bundle up. We'll head out."

Their walk was slow, taking about thirty minutes. Meg was thrilled to see them, she and Mary had enjoyed a quiet morning with brunch and gifts they opened before Meg's tree in the parlor.

"I love my beautiful hat," Meg said to Lindsay, "and I love my warm scarf and gloves," she said to Evan, hugging them both together, forcing them nearer to one another. "These cookies smell divine. Mary and I will have some later with tea."

"Are you making dinner today?" Evan asked. "Because we have tons of leftovers - you'd be more than welcome to join us, you and Mary."

"Thank you, Dear," she said. "That's very sweet of you, but Mary has invited her brother and his wife over for a light supper later. Neither of us have seen them in years, not since Mike died. I think I'll stay and visit with them – you two have a cozy day together."

Evan looked at Lindsay and she glanced at him. They both smiled at Meg, ever the matchmaker.

"Will you have something hot to drink? I have cider, and there's always coffee and tea."

Lindsay put her hand on her stomach. "Evan made pancakes this morning and I'm stuffed. Thank you though."

"I'm all set too," Evan said. "Maybe we'll be ready for something hot when we get home." He looked at Lindsay and she was aware that his eyes were on her face. She stood and started to button her coat.

They said Merry Christmas then left for their walk back. At about the halfway mark, they left the beach area and walked across the street to Lindsay's lonely looking little cottage. Lindsay took a key from her pocket and opened the door.

"I feel very bad," Evan said. "I should have thought to buy your Gray Gull a wreath, especially since I'm the reason you're away from here."

Lindsay looked around – it seemed so small now after living for months at Evan's house. "That's okay," she said. "I'll have next year here."

That statement hung in the air like an anchor on a chain. It made Lindsay feel alone and sad to think of being away from Evan's home and without him. She loved her cottage, she would enjoy it again, but the joy of being there would not diminish her longing for being with Evan to raise their baby.

Evan looked around at the cottage, cozy in every corner with touches from Lindsay. She thought he looked sad. He walked to the mantle where he picked up and looked closely at a photo of Lindsay as a child with her parents. He looked at her and she thought she could detect watery eyes in this strong man.

"They look nice," he said.

Lindsay nodded. They were nice – they had been wonderful.

"I'd offer to make coffee or tea," she said, "but it's a little chilly in here. I have the heat set to just sixty – we might be better off to get back to your place."

"Let's go," he said, "when we get home, I'll beat you at a game of some kind. We have about everything you could think of in the attic."

"Maybe a game and an old movie," Lindsay said as they walked.

"Maybe a game and an old movie and some cookies and coffee," he said.

Lindsay smiled. "Okay."

Chapter Eighteen

Christmas was unforgettable to Lindsay. With her parents and grandparents the holiday had always been filled with bright lights, good food, thoughtful gifts, and oceans of love. The Christmases that followed the accident, living with her aunt and uncle, were filled with activity and new traditions. This Christmas day with Evan was different from anything she could have planned. It was quiet but layered with meaningful gifts and a sense of contentment. More than she could have imagined, coupled with expecting the most sensational child in the world, this holiday was pure magic.

Two days before New Year's Eve Evan asked Lindsay what she was doing to celebrate.

"I don't know," she said honestly. She had just arrived home from work and had not thought about doing anything in particular for New Year's Eve. It was a holiday she preferred to skip – loud noises, crazy hats, and too much drinking.

"Are you interested in going to a party? They're having some kind of celebration at the Lighthouse Lounge. I was thinking of going for a while."

Lindsay remembered seeing him there with a blonde. There would certainly be single women there hoping to make a connection - she could envision Evan having no trouble at all meeting and hooking up with someone.

"I think I'll pass," she said. "I'm not much for these parties on New Year's."

"Okay. But will you do something? Maybe dine with Meg? Sara and Ben are going off again. You'd be here alone."

Lindsay looked up at him from her seat in the kitchen. "No, I'll have Adele and Charlie. I'll be fine."

Evan looked at her and seemed frustrated. When she went back to looking through his mother's old recipe file, he walked to his workroom. Lindsay wanted to sob. A new year approaching and she would be alone at that wonderful moment when old meets new - no one to kiss.

When New Year's Eve came, Evan stopped in to the living room where Lindsay sat reading with her tea. Dressed in a dark casual suit, he looked incredibly handsome - his cologne was light yet intoxicating.

"Are you sure you'll be all right?" he asked.

"Positive," she said. She nearly added that she hoped he'd have a good time, but she thought that would be a dishonest statement.

"Okay then," he said. "Good night, Lindsay."

She waved and smiled, choking back the words and the tears – then her eyes went back to her book. When the door closed behind him, she put the book down in her lap and covered her face with her hands. Tears streaked down toward her lips and she wiped them quickly away. She had to get a hold on this – it was coming to an end. Keith was getting better and would soon be able to take care of his son. She looked around the room at everything there, memories created by two wonderful people who gave life to a wonderful man. It was sad and ironic, the two of them only children who had lost their parents. It made them kindred spirits in a way, forcing them to pave the way for a new path. Lindsay thought about Tess, how drastically unfair her death was. She thought too of Kathy with her little Audra. Lindsay stiffened her back and finished her tea. She convinced herself that she needed to be strong – in the long run, you had yourself to lean on – everyone else had their own life to live.

Before midnight, Lindsay went upstairs to bed. She did not want to think about where Evan was or who he might be with. At ten minutes before twelve, she heard a light knock at her door and Evan's voice saying her name. She wiped away tears and decided to pretend sleep. She stayed there staring at a darkened ceiling for a long time before she closed her eyes and slept.

With morning light, she squinted against the brightness from the window and turned on her side to escape it. The little clock on her night stand informed her that it was nearly eight o'clock, late for her to be getting up. Reluctantly, she pushed the covers away and stood, then made her bed and dressed. She was not anxious to see Evan – she was very tired of the pretense. As sad as she knew she would feel leaving this house and him; it was inevitable.

Downstairs, she found Adele and Charlie playing with one of the ornaments off the little tree. She laughed at them and then made herself a cup of tea. Thinking that she had the house to herself, she walked barefoot into the living room and sat down near where she'd left her book. Moments later, the door to Evan's workroom opened and he sat down across from her.

"Early evening last night?" he asked.

"No, actually I just got in," she said with a hint of teasing.

"Really? I saw your car here – did someone pick you up?" He did not sound like he believed her, but was testing her anyway.

"Oh," she went on, "I was picked up in a limo – a big silver one, with bells and streamers all over it - quite something."

"And," he said, "the evening must have been pretty wild, I see you lost your shoes."

Lindsay looked down at her bare feet and wiggled her toes, saying nothing.

"Well," he said as he reached in his pocket, "I have something for you." He handed her a small black box and she accepted it tentatively.

"What is it?" she asked.

"You'll see when you open it."

Lindsay looked at him and then raised the lid to find a beautiful antique cameo brooch. Nearly speechless she asked, "Why?"

Evan smiled. "Because you deserve it - it was my mother's. Before she died, she asked me to choose carefully those who would appreciate some of her things. She wasn't a diamond lady – she liked cameos. There are others in her jewelry box, but I like this one best. I want you to have it."

"But we're going to be parting soon. Don't you want to keep this for the future? I'm overwhelmed with this, Evan, but I don't think I can accept it."

"Please," he said. "I want you to have it. The face on that piece reminds me of you. I could never give it to someone else."

She held the cameo in her hands for a long time, staring at the carved profile. It was beautiful and sentimental – a meaningful gift from her husband.

"Thank you," she said. "I'll treasure this always."

Evan looked pleased. "Back to work tomorrow for you - I'll be here working. It's kind of strange being a civilian now – the Navy was a chunk of my life."

"Did you like being part of the military?"

"I did. I made good friends and I was able to get some needed schooling while actually being useful. After my father died, I'd had it. I needed to get out of Cliff Point for a while. Coming back here for the last several months of my enlistment was great – it allowed me to transition with a slow pace, and it made me understand that this is where I want to spend my life. I questioned that sometimes – I wasn't sure I could come back to the place where both of my parents died."

Lindsay nodded. "I had that issue with living in my parents' home. Peter, my husband, wanted to be there. It was hard to touch their furniture, to look at their desks and remember them in the kitchen eating oatmeal every morning. They were very health conscious, unless there was chocolate cake in the house." Lindsay smiled and Evan did too.

"Since this is the first day of a new year, how about if we drive someplace and have lunch or an early dinner. It's not bad out today – any interest in a trek to Pemaquid Point? The restaurant there is open – I checked."

Lindsay felt elated. "I'd love to go to Pemaquid. I'll take my camera, you've made it sound fascinating."

Evan nodded. "It is fascinating – you're going to want to paint it sometime. It's beyond spectacular. Dress warm, and wear shoes. The wind up there can take it up a notch and you'll be glad for an extra warmth in the way of a heavy jacket, scarf, and gloves. A hat wouldn't hurt either."

An hour later, they drove along the coast until they reached their beautiful destination. "This is it," he said as they pulled up to a grouping of cottages, the restaurant overlooking the sea, and a lighthouse. It was magnificent. Lindsay started to get out of the car when Evan opened her door and reached for her gloved hand.

"Come on," he said. "It's too cold for us to stay out here long. Come and look at the rocks and the surf, then we'll get in out of this wind for some lunch."

Lindsay held on to her hat and looked in awe at the incredible sight before her. "I've never seen anything this wonderful before. The beaches near Boston and the Cape tend to be sandy and flat with the occasional dunes. These rocks are just wonderful – you're right, I'll want to come back to paint this scenery. I am completely thrilled to be seeing this. Thank you, Evan."

They sat inside the restaurant with hot coffee and fried clam dinners, their eyes fastened to the activity outside. Gulls dipped and soared over the rocks, the wind ruffled their feathers and at times sent them off course. Monhegan Island was pointed out to her by Evan and she looked at that distant place as being peaceful and a little mysterious. She imagined what it would be like to live isolated on an island at this time of year.

"I've been out there in the summer," he said thoughtfully, "long ago with my parents. It's a great place."

"Is there a ferry?" Lindsay asked.

"There's a mail boat. Not an advisable trip for this time of year, but definitely a great way to spend a day in the summer."

Lindsay looked out to the crashing waves and thought about what the summer would bring. How would she explain having a baby? Could she possibly remain in Cliff Point?

When she looked back at him, she found that he was looking at her and it was an awkward moment. He looked toward the sea – neither of them spoke and then they continued with their meals and coffee.

"This has been a great treat," she said. "The food is delicious and I could sit here forever watching this incredible show. I noticed there's a gift shop here. I wouldn't mind browsing a little to see if I could find a book or two about this area, and maybe some little trinket to bring back to Meg - maybe a piece of glass for one of her kitchen windows."

"That's a good idea. Maybe I'll pick up something like that for Sara and Ben, and maybe you'd like something too. I noticed you have some glass pieces in your cottage – they look nice with the light from outside shining through. But before that, would you like dessert or more coffee?"

"I'd love more coffee," Lindsay said. "It feels good to be drinking it again, but no dessert – I'm too full."

"What was going on with you and coffee? When I first met you, it was your beverage of choice. Suddenly, you switched to tea."

Lindsay squirmed just a bit. "I don't know. I just felt like having tea for a while. I love coffee – I'm enjoying it so much today and having this scenery to look at doesn't hurt either."

Evan ordered another round of coffee for each of them and a slice of blueberry pie which he coaxed her to share. She took one bite, agreed it was delicious, then said that the hot coffee would be all she could handle.

After more than a half hour sipping their coffee and watching the sea, Evan and Lindsay walked into the gift shop. Almost immediately Lindsay found a book on Pemaquid Point – she also found a children's book on seashore creatures and beautiful shells - she would buy them both. Evan called to her when he located disk-like pieces of glass with thin nylon strings attached to hang in a window or from a place where light would enhance the colors.

"I love this blue one," Lindsay said holding up a piece with an embossed sea gull design, "I need that for my Gray Gull. And this purple piece is beautiful – I think that would be nice for Meg."

Evan looked over her shoulder at the selections. "What do you think about that green one with the sailing ship on it for Sara and Ben?"

"Perfect," Lindsay said.

When they were heading home in the car, Evan asked for whom she purchased the children's book. "Is that for your friend's little girl?"

"Maybe," Lindsay said softly, "I just liked it."

He smiled and when he glanced over at her, he noticed that her eyes were half closed. He was quiet as he drove and when they arrived back in Cliff Point and he turned off the car's engine, Lindsay was surprised to find herself home.

"I'm sorry," she said. "I'm not a very good companion for falling asleep."

"Don't worry about it," he said. "Some days we need a little nap."

In the house, Evan lit a fire in the hearth and asked Lindsay what her evening looked like. "I'm expected someplace for a while later," he said. "Will you be okay on your own?"

Lindsay said that she would, but she wondered where he was going. Being New Year's Day, it had to have been a social rather than work related evening. And then she questioned herself about why she was giving the subject any thought at all – he did not belong to her in any real way. The trip to Pemaquid Point had been wonderful – she would hold on to that memory.

When he left around seven, he was wearing gray slacks and a black shirt. Lindsay watched from her sofa seat in the living room as he slipped into a sport jacket, threw a scarf around his neck, and left. She stared at the door long after it had closed behind him – his departure left her with a feeling of emptiness and she reminded herself again, it was useless to have an emotional attachment to a temporary issue.

After reading a few more pages of her book and finishing her coffee, Lindsay looked at the decorations. Sara and Ben would be home tomorrow – maybe this would be a good time to start taking the garlands down and tossing the holly and balsam bouquets away. It made her sad to think of discarding Christmas, especially this one, when she found herself in love.

Little by little, greens and ornaments were taken down and placed where they belonged. She stripped the tree of its ornaments, carefully placing them in their containers. The stark tree, darkened without its lights, looked forlorn standing near the hearth. With the living room back to normal except for the tree itself, Lindsay went in to the kitchen. It was now nearly nine o'clock. She checked Adele and Charlie for food and water, then looked at the cheerful little tree. Tears came to her eyes and she decided that she'd had enough for one day. The tree would stay for now.

Restless, she went to Evan's study and switched on the TV. She flipped channels to see what she might watch and found a program on designing houses – she thought Evan would like this. When she woke up, it was after eleven. Evan was still not home. Lindsay locked the door and made sure that the hearth fire was cold before going upstairs to bed.

Chapter Nineteen

Over the next few days, Lindsay worked with her boss to catalogue new technical additions from the government to their library. By the end of each day, she felt well, but eager to get home.

One morning when Evan indicated that he was meeting with a client that evening, and would not be home until after nine, Lindsay decided that she would go to her cottage after work. She lit a fire in the hearth and made herself some tea. While she was there, she dusted a bit and took from her purse the blue glass piece from Pemaquid Point. The fact that it depicted a sea gull was perfect – she hung it in a window across from the hearth where the brilliance of the deep blue could most be appreciated.

She walked around in her small space, thinking what a wonderful day that had been. Since then, it seemed Evan was just a little evasive – he'd spoken to her, but not at any length. What had happened to change what they'd shared over Christmas?

It wasn't until a few days later that things became clear. Kathy and Deb sat with her having lunch when Ted McNee came along and greeted them cheerfully.

"Hey," he said, "Isn't it great news about Keith Hatherly? The guy is doing terrific."

Lindsay looked up to Ted's face. "What do you mean? Has something changed?"

"Evan didn't tell you? Keith is out of rehab – he's back living in base quarters with his son. Everything is good – no more worries about that aunt in Missouri."

Deb and Kathy commented on the good news – Lindsay said nothing.

Why had Evan not told her about this? She felt stunned – everything was ending. Maybe, she thought, he didn't know how to tell her to leave, to go back to her own place.

The next day was Saturday. Lindsay was told by Sara and Ben that Evan had business that morning and wouldn't be back until later in the day. She drank some tea, decided against breakfast, and went upstairs to her room. There, she sat down on her bed and thought about what to do. After a few minutes, she packed her belongings. Each item she placed in a carton seemed like a giant step away from love. This had not been an expected outcome – this was heartbreaking.

By noon, Lindsay had packed and had taken her possessions to her car. She spoke briefly to Sara and Ben about her decision. "There's no need for the pretense any longer," she said. "I'll talk to Evan at some point about Charlie. I'm hoping he'll agree to leave him with his mother, but if not, I'll gladly take him. No matter what, they will both need to see a veterinarian soon."

"Oh, yes," Sara agreed. "I don't want to go through partings any more. We definitely need to take care of them soon."

"I'll miss you," Lindsay said as she hugged Sara and Ben, then she knelt down to pet Adele and Charlie. "I'll miss you too," she said.

"Will you come by and see us sometimes?" Sara said with a quiver in her voice. "It's going to seem so lonely without you. We've loved having you in the house."

Lindsay looked at the two dear faces. "I'm sure we'll see one another." Her eyes scanned the kitchen she loved and she thought the tears would begin if she didn't get out of there. "We'll stay in touch," she said with a trace of a smile and then she turned and walked toward her car.

Turning the key in the lock to her door, Lindsay stepped into the large room and felt motionless. She looked at the cold hearth, the light from an overcast day cascading through her windows – it was all gray. She placed her suitcase down on the floor to her right and decided to collect the carton from her backset later. She closed the door and walked in. After turning the thermostat up, she placed logs and kindling in the fireplace and prodded it to provide warmth and light by sticking bits of twigs and paper in with the wood. Within a few minutes, the cottage became warm and welcoming. She was home.

It was nearly seven that evening when Lindsay decided that she'd put the kettle on for tea and change into some warm pajamas, slippers, and a robe. With tea and a slice of toast with peanut butter for her supper, she sat down and watched the gently leaping flames in the hearth. She thought about the flickering of flames being like the ticking of clocks – did everything have a heart? Was the essence of life in absolutely everything? Was all of this her hopes for spirits living on in inanimate objects? She didn't know. She felt sad and she knew that she was hoping, searching. She leaned back on the sofa and pulled an afghan over her legs, then she slid further down and rested her head against a pillow. How long, she wondered, before I feel the baby move? At least another month, maybe two. Lindsay smiled thinking of how that sensation would feel – a little life moving around inside of her.

After ten o'clock, she woke up and was annoyed with herself for falling asleep. She switched on the TV and made more tea. She made herself another slice of toast and started a grocery list to include apples and grapes. She was writing down perishable items when she heard a knock at the door. She glanced at the clock on her mantle; it was ten-twenty. Who would be out visiting at that hour?

She stood and walked to the door, but before opening it, she called out to ask who was there.

"It's me," came Evan's strong voice.

Lindsay opened the door and found his tall, lanky frame standing straight before her. Without an invitation, he brushed by her and walked into the room. He looked around for a moment, then as she closed the door against the cold, he faced her, his hands tucked into the pockets of his bomber jacket.

"What's going on?" he asked with an angry tone.

Lindsay began to feel her defense system at work. "I don't think you have any right to ask that question."

Evan unzipped his jacket, tossed it carelessly on a chair and sat down on the middle cushion of her sofa.

Lindsay moved his jacket just a bit, then sat down in that chair and looked straight at him.

"Why are you here?" he asked.

"Are you kidding me, Evan? When were you going to tell me that Keith was now okay? Why did it take Sara and Ben to tell me? I think I've been pretty patient and fair about all of this. What happened to you being square with me?"

Evan moved his eyes from her face to the hearth then back at her again. "I would have told you. I was waiting for the right time."

"What time would have been right, Evan? I've put my own life on hold and I've made a lot of adjustments. When were you going to tell me that I had my life back?"

Evan stood, rubbed his brow and walked to the hearth. He poked at the wood with a piece of kindling then threw another log on the fire. When he turned around to look at Lindsay, his eyes had a softness which had not been there when he first arrived.

"I'm sorry," he said. "You're right – I should have told you as soon as I found out that Keith was back in base housing."

Lindsay kept her eyes to his. "Why didn't you?"

Evan walked back to the sofa and sat down. "It was Christmas. I didn't want everything to change right in the middle of our plans. We had Christmas Eve's buffet with Meg and the Phillips. We had the trees. And that reminds me," he said as he sat forward, "that little tree in the kitchen is still up."

"I took the decorations from the big tree, and I left the garlands and bouquets of holly and balsam outside the back door. Are you telling me that you can't manage to take care of the little kitchen tree?"

"Yeah, I guess I can."

"Good," Lindsay said. "And while we're discussing the kitchen, I wanted to talk to you about Adele and Charlie. Charlie could come here to live with me as planned, but I think Adele would miss him, and that he would miss her as well. Would you allow them to stay together?"

Evan nodded. "As long as we get them to the vet soon – I have no problem with them remaining together. I'll make an appointment for them this week."

Lindsay agreed and was very relieved that he'd taken the suggestion so well.

"Well," he said, "I suppose you're tired and I should get going so you can sleep."

Evan glanced from her pretty face to a chess board on a corner shelf. "That's a nice looking chess set," he said.

"It was my father's. He had an interest in the Civil War – all of those pieces are of generals, horses, and such. Do you play?"

"Yes, do you?"

"I haven't in a long time, but yes, I play."

"I haven't in a long time either. Maybe we could have a game some time."

"Maybe," she said.

Evan stood. "Look, I'm going to get out of here and let you get some rest, but I want you to know that these past few months have been appreciated. Keith wants to take us out to dinner some night – he's amazed at what we did – at what you did. I've been friends with him for a long time. You don't even know him and yet you did him this enormous favor, putting yourself completely out. Thank you – from Keith and from me."

Lindsay stood and walked with him toward the door, staring down at her slippered feet, then up to his handsome face. "I'm glad it kept Sean here."

Evan looked at her as he slipped his jacket on and zipped it up. "Goodnight, Lindsay."

"Goodnight."

When the door was closed and locked, Lindsay could hear the engine of Evan's car as he pulled away toward his home. She looked at the cottage she had once thought of as the most perfect of places – now she was divided. Evan's home had become a place to love too.

Chapter Twenty

For the next few days Lindsay felt depressed. The excitement of finding herself in love and living in Evan's wonderful home was fading. She could feel it all slipping away, that warm and wonderful sense of family. Having Sara and Ben around was a comfort, and she missed the cats too.

When Meg called to invite her for dinner, Lindsay was hesitant. What could they possibly have to discuss? The holidays were over – no more parties. The issue with Keith and Sean was settled – no more reason to entwine her life with Evan's. There was the joy of expecting a baby, but she could not share that – not yet. If Evan were to learn of his child, he might do "the right thing" and suggest that they stay married. She wanted marriage for no other reason than for love – she'd made that mistake with Peter, settling in with him to once again have her own home. After a bit of coaxing, Meg convinced Lindsay to join her for dinner.

"Are you glad to be back in your own little place?" Meg asked over coffee and dessert.

"I love the cottage – it's everything I need."

Meg listened to her young friend's words but noted the expression on her face – she thought Lindsay seemed a bit sad. "But is it everything you want?"

Lindsay placed her cup down on its saucer. "It's the right place for me at this time."

"Have you talked to Evan about separating? Is the annulment going through?"

"Not yet. He told me he'd take care of it, but I've heard nothing. I don't care – it's not like I have someone waiting in the wings to sweep me away. I'm sure it will happen in time."

"How are you and your friends doing at work? I'm sure you all miss Tess."

"It's still surreal to us. Of the four of us, Tess was the live wire – it was she who made us laugh and told us the truth about ourselves. In spite of some of her own problems, she was always in tune with ours. I can't believe she's gone. It's going to take us a long time not to feel so much pain with her loss."

"It does take time, Dear. You know that as well as I do. Losing your parents and Peter must have been shocking each time – and losing Mike was a nightmare. I still wake up sometimes with the hope that it didn't really happen."

Lindsay thought about her feelings for Evan. She was discovering that when she now opened her eyes in the morning, she had less enthusiasm for getting out of bed. At Evan's home, there was that wonderfully warm kitchen and the prospect of seeing him.

"What kinds of things do you have in mind for this winter? Winters in Maine can be long."

Lindsay shrugged her shoulders and smiled. "I'm kind of just existing at the moment. I have a few things I'll get to, such as my painting. I have about ten books I'd like to read. I don't know – I manage to keep occupied. What do you do in the winter here? You must have a plan after all these years."

Meg laughed. "You'd think so, but no. I keep busy with the volunteer work at the hospital and, of course, I have Mary to chat with most of the time, but like you, I have no particular agenda. I like a good book too – I'll try and get some reading time in."

Lindsay nodded. "It actually sounds relaxing – a nice fire in the hearth, hot tea, and a good book. I find myself looking toward spring and summer. I did nothing with my yard last summer – I hadn't been here that long, but I want to make up for what I didn't accomplish. I'm thinking of planting some bulbs, maybe tulips, and I would love to grow Wisteria and maybe lilacs. I love my cottage interior, but it's exciting to think of working outside when the weather permits."

"Do you miss him?" Meg asked out of the blue.

Lindsay looked from the hearth to Meg. "Who?"

"Evan. Do you miss him?"

Lindsay sat further back in her seat. "He was interesting to live with for a few months."

Meg smiled. "I'm sure. He's a very bright young man, and not hard to look at either."

"I didn't notice."

"Your nose is going to grow," Meg teased.

Lindsay gave in to a smile. "Tell me about the hospital. I thought it was nice, very friendly the day I was there with Kathy and Audra."

"It is nice – I think it's great for a small facility. The base has a bigger hospital than the town does, but sometimes they actually work in unison. It's a good relationship."

"Do you ever work with the infants?"

"No," Meg shook her head. "The volunteers in that department are usually child-bearing age. I'm mostly in post-operative areas, doing more clerical work than anything directly with patients. I like it though. I'm helpful to them and they give me a purpose."

"This seems like a wonderful place to raise children. Aside from the natural beauty, the residents here seem so accepting of newcomers like me."

"Part of that is the mind-set of the residents – they're used to the military coming and going, and some of us staying. We're a very good partnership. I was military, Mary was Cliff Point – we found a wonderful friendship in one another, and that's not unique to us."

Lindsay stood. Approaching nearly four months of pregnancy, she was beginning to feel the waistband on her slacks to be snug. "I think that although this time together was wonderful and I thank you so much for having me, I will go home and settle in. But, will you dine with me at the cottage next time? I'll make a real dinner – no grilled cheese, I promise."

Meg walked with Lindsay to the coat closet and the front door. "Grilled cheese would suit me fine. I would love an evening in your Gray Gull."

Walking into her own little home no longer gave Lindsay the thrill it once had. The place hadn't changed – she had. She pulled off gloves and hung her coat then walked directly to the hearth which she lit. From there she moved to the kitchen and placed a kettle on for tea. The next step was to her bedroom where she traded her warm slacks and sweater for pajamas and a robe. Not fond of slippers, she pushed them aside and pulled warm socks over her feet. Lindsay was glad to be able to provide herself with some physical comfort – the emotional part of her was in turmoil.

Shortly after she had poured herself a cup of hot tea, there was a substantial knock at her door. She sat for a moment – it was after eight o'clock. She stood and walked to the front entrance asking who was there.

"It's Evan."

Lindsay unlocked the door and opened it to a stern face and a cold wind.

"May I come in?"

Lindsay stepped aside. "Yes, of course. I just made tea, would you like some?"

Evan rubbed his hands together. "Yeah, that would be good."

Lindsay looked at his red face. "Did you walk here?"

"Yes."

"In the cold and dark? Why?"

"I felt like going for a walk - I found myself here. I saw your lights and the smell of your fire drifted out toward the sea – it seemed like an invitation. How have you been?"

She wanted to blurt out that she was terrible – that she missed him like nothing she'd imagined and that this was a fulfillment of her longing just to be in the same room with him again.

"I'm okay," she said.

"It's been a while. You should really come by and see the cats you know."

Lindsay turned her back to him and smiled as she went for his tea. "Yes, I miss them. And I miss Sara and Ben too."

Evan accepted the mug of hot tea when she returned and looked at her. He did not ask the question, but it was there in his eyes and she ignored it. They were quiet for a few moments, each of them watching the flickering flames in shades of blue and tangerine.

"How's work?" he asked as he turned his gaze to her.

Lindsay met his eyes. "It's good. I like my boss, she's very straight forward – you always know what to expect from her. And she's smart."

"Is this something you see yourself doing long term?"

Lindsay looked pensive. "I suppose I could, but I've always hoped for something more."

"Like what?"

Lindsay knew exactly what she wanted to say, but she knew to be careful, not to seem anxious or suggestive. "Well, work-wise, I like what I'm doing. It's very close to what I was doing in Boston as a research librarian. But work isn't enough – I'd like to think that I'll have a family some day."

Evan looked at her and sipped his hot tea.

"Any chance we could dig that chess game out and have a go at it?"

"Now?"

"Is it too late?"

Lindsay's eyes went to the clock on her mantle – it was nearly nine. "No, I guess we could have a game."

"Great," he said as he stood, deposited his tea on a table, and went to retrieve the chess set. He placed it on the coffee table in front of the sofa.

"Wouldn't it be better if we played on the table by the window?"

"Not unless you'd rather. I thought I'd pull a chair over and you can sit on the sofa – that way, we can be close to the fire while we play."

"Okay," Lindsay said and wondered if she should go and change from pajamas to slacks and a sweater.

As she stood motionless deciding, Evan looked up at her from the chair he'd chosen. "Everything all right?"

"I was thinking of getting into some jeans or something."

"Lindsay," he said with a little smile, "think how many times you walked around looking like a three-year old at my house. You practically lived in pajamas. Why the sudden modesty? You have more clothes on now than with regular clothes."

"I didn't look like a three-year old. Did you really think I looked like a three-year old?"

Evan set up the game. "Sort of. Come on, I have a black piece and a white piece behind my back. Which hand?"

"Left," she said.

"Ah, you get the white guys. Okay. Come on- sit down. Let me show you how to win at this game."

Lindsay thought that he already had won at this game, but she wasn't thinking of chess.

Two hours later after each of them had made clever and calculated moves, they reached a stalemate. Lindsay sat back on the sofa pleased that she hadn't forgotten how to be cautious and cunning – this had been fun.

"This was interesting," Evan said as he gave her a long look and then slipped his arms into his jacket. "We'll have to do this again soon

– maybe at my place next time."

"Wait," she said. "It's eleven o'clock. You aren't walking home at this hour, are you? I'll get some clothes on and drive you."

"Lindsay," he said as he placed his hands on her upper arms, "I'll be fine. It's less than a mile."

"If you don't want me to drive you, take my car. You can return it in the morning and then I can drive you home."

Evan laughed. "I'll be fine. Look, it will take me about fifteen minutes. As soon as I get to the house, I'll give you a quick call. Does that work?"

"Not really."

Evan opened the door. "I'll call you in about fifteen or twenty minutes." He smiled at her and left.

Lindsay washed the tea mugs, brushed her teeth, and waited. Just as she had decided to panic, the phone rang.

"I'm home," he said. "I had a great time tonight. Thanks for having me. Goodnight, Lindsay."

"Goodnight," she said and hoped it had sounded like more than a whisper to him.

Lindsay turned out the lights and was satisfied that the hearth was darkening and safe to leave while she went to bed. She lay in her room, a thick quilt pulled up to her chin. This had been a very good night.

Chapter Twenty-One

A full week went by and Lindsay did not see or hear from Evan. She had dined with Meg, but his name had not been mentioned. At work, she kept busy and enjoyed the companionship she'd found in Kathy and Deb - they talked about Tess frequently. They also learned to laugh and to mention crazy little antics Tess had instigated without dissolving into tears. They were supportive of one another.

Lindsay also remained close to Louisa Phillips. She liked the fact that Louisa was not originally from Cliff Point – it helped Lindsay to believe that this wonderful ocean-side town could become her forever home. She wanted that – for herself and for her baby. But how? How could she possibly live where the father of her child was well known and quite possibly indifferent. This thought was with her constantly.

On a cold Saturday morning Lindsay was outside gathering a few logs to bring in for the hearth when Evan's car pulled up to her house. She stopped to look at him walking toward her.

"Hi," he said. "Let me give you a hand with this." She had three logs in her arms, he picked up another six. When he deposited them inside, he told her to stay in while he selected a few more to leave by the hearth. With an ample pile stashed in a cubby hole provided for the wood, Lindsay thanked him – all of that would have taken her three or four trips outside.

"No problem," he said. "And, I wanted to ask you if you could join Keith and me tomorrow for dinner. He wants to thank us. I told him there was no need, but he wants to know you and thank you in person."

"I guess that would be okay," Lindsay said. "Where and what time?"

"He wants to take us to Damariscotta – there's a place there he favors. He thought around three – would that work for you?"

"Yes, that's fine. Are we going with him or should I drive there on my own?"

"I'll pick you up. I think Keith is taking Sean, so we'll meet them there. I know the place he chose. It's nice, you'll like it."

"Okay, so what time will you pick me up?"

"How about two-fifteen? That will give us plenty of time."

Lindsay nodded and seemed quiet.

"Everything okay with you these days?" he asked.

"Oh, sure. Yes, everything's fine."

"All right then, I'll see you tomorrow at two-fifteen."

Lindsay closed the door softly as he went to his car. This was agonizing. Sometimes she saw him, sometimes she didn't. She'd become accustomed to seeing him every day when she lived at his house. She sighed and walked to her bedroom to check on at what she had that still fit and didn't show her little bump that was getting more noticeable every day. She found a soft jersey skirt in deep brown with a matching top. It was loose and would allow her to deceive him for at least a while longer. Within another month, this pregnancy was going to be tricky – Deb, Kathy, Louisa, and Meg were going to notice fairly soon.

The next day Evan showed up at exactly the right time. Lindsay was feeling wonderful now and looked radiant. As he watched her move around the cottage collecting her purse and slipping her feet into dark brown shoes with a one-inch heel, he seemed to be studying her.

"You look nice," he said.

Lindsay allowed a faint smile to widen her lips – could he be any more stingy with his compliments?

"Thank you," she said. "You look nice too."

They were quiet at first in the car. Then Evan asked, "So, what have you been doing with yourself?"

"Just keeping up with work during the day - I see Meg and Louisa sometimes. Some evenings I paint."

"That sounds relaxing. Since I left the Navy, I've been incredibly busy. When you're in the service, your life is very directed – when you're in charge of yourself, you need to be good at time management. I'm trying to get a handle on that."

Lindsay understood – she recalled thinking of how her parents had arranged everything in her life and then they were gone. Living with her aunt, uncle, and cousins was completely different, not nearly so orderly. And then there had been Peter, who wanted everything in his life to be punctual and predictable. Living on her own, while filled with freedom, was often lonely.

"What was he like?" Evan asked as if reading her mind.

"Who?"

"Your husband."

Lindsay thought about how to explain Peter. "He was intelligent and ambitious. He was becoming known as a powerful attorney in Boston – everyone knew who he was – he was well liked."

Evan nodded but said nothing.

Lindsay felt that Meg had probably told him more and decided to be completely honest. "I feel guilty sometimes when I think of this, but had Peter lived, I don't think we'd have stayed together. We were fine as individuals, but not such a good pair."

Evan nodded. "It happens," he said softly.

"What about you? You must have had some past relationships, or even present interests."

Evan smiled as he navigated the curves of the coastal road. "I've had a few interesting relationships. Being in the military, it's hard – you move around a lot."

"No one special?" Lindsay asked.

"Once," he said, "but it was impossible."

Lindsay swallowed and wasn't sure she wanted to know more.

When he began to continue with the story, Lindsay found herself listening intently.

"Before here, I was stationed in California after coming back from Asia. I was in this little bar one night and saw this blonde who didn't seem like the bar type. She looked frail, kind of sad. I walked over to her and asked if I could buy her a drink or even a coffee. She accepted. She started to tell me, at times tearfully, about her life. I felt helpless. I met her a few times after that – we just talked – no wild dates. She told me that she was married and had a little boy. She was dying."

Lindsay felt stunned. "How old was she? She must have been young."

"She was twenty-six."

"What about her husband and little boy? Did they know?"

"Her husband knew, not her son. He was only three or four at the time. Anyway, she had this crazy idea – she wanted to convince her husband that she wasn't worthy of all his sorrow concerning her illness, so she went out evenings – she tried to make him think she'd become a bar-fly. He didn't buy it, but it didn't stop her from trying."

"What happened to her?"

"She died."

Lindsay shook her head. "How awful." And then she asked, "Had you fallen in love with her?"

Evan took his time answering that question. "I loved her, but I did not fall in love with her. Once I understood what was going on with her husband and her health, I became her friend."

"That's so sad. Did you ever meet her husband and child?"

"Yes," he said, "the girl I've been telling you about was Mary Ann Hatherly, Keith's wife."

Lindsay felt overwhelmed with emotion. "That's how you came to know Keith?"

"Actually I'd known him for a few years. Not well, and I certainly didn't know about the situation he was living with. Being in the Navy together – we'd had a drink a couple of times among other friends and I'd worked with him briefly at one point."

Lindsay wiped a stray tear from her face. "No wonder it was important to you to help keep Keith and Sean together – you understood their loss."

"And," Evan said as they pulled up to the restaurant, "I didn't want them to lose any more – they'd been through enough. I know you met Keith at Meg's party, but I'm glad you're going to have this chance to see him again, and to meet Sean. I think that once Keith gets on his feet securely, they'll be shipping out to Florida, and then in a few years, retirement. Maybe back in Cliff Point with us."

Lindsay took Evan's hand as he stood at her opened car door. How easily he'd said *with us* in reference to living in Cliff Point.

The late afternoon meal and meeting with Keith and Sean turned out to be wonderful. Lindsay admired Keith and found Sean to be an adorable child, bright and happy.

When they were leaving the restaurant after five, Sean walked to Evan's car beside Lindsay and took her hand. "Thank you for saving us," he said. "I'm really glad Uncle Evan has you."

Lindsay's eyes filled with tears as she bent forward to hug Sean.

Evan and Keith stood watching the tender scene, smiles on their faces.

The ride home to Cliff Point in the dark part of the day was in silence. Evan seemed to understand that Lindsay needed the quiet time to absorb all that she had learned that day. What Lindsay came to realize was that life was precarious and meant to be lived as well as one could. She had suffered her losses, but accepted that she was not singled out to know sorrow.

Chapter Twenty-Two

On a bitterly cold and snowy morning in late January, Lindsay looked outside at the weather and thought she needed to take a day off from work for the first time. She made tea for herself and when she knew that Laura Sinnott would be there, she called to say that she would not be in. Replacing the phone on its receiver, Lindsay had a strong urge to call her boss back and simply resign. This situation was going to be impossible. She decided that rather than make her announcement over the phone, she would talk with Mrs. Sinnott tomorrow. There were no other options – she would pack some of her clothes and a few other items and go away. Maybe when the baby was eight or nine months, or a year old, she would return to Cliff Point and say nothing of the father's identity. She could not reconcile with the thought that she wouldn't return and that she wouldn't raise this child here where he or she had been conceived.

With a blazing fire in the hearth and a cup of tea nearby, she began to pack what clothes she thought would fit her for awhile. Occasionally, she stopped and allowed the tears to flow, then she would look around and think about what she would take with her and what she would leave in the cottage until her return.

With a large, nearly full carton on her sofa, she placed the last item on top before sealing it with tape when she heard a knock at the door. It was just after noon and Lindsay thought it was the mailman. When she opened the door and was about to tell him that she needed to make other arrangements for her mail, she found Evan standing before her.

"Are you all right?" he asked. "I saw your car here instead of at work – I was a little concerned."

"I'm okay," she said trying to block his view of the sofa and the carton.

"What are you doing? Why are you home?" He looked around her and saw the carton. "What's going on?" he said as he invited himself through the doorway and in by the hearth.

Lindsay looked down at her feet in heavy dark gray socks, then she met his eyes. "I'm going away for awhile."

Evan looked speechless. After a moment he said, "Why? You told me once that it would take something huge to make you leave Cliff Point. What has happened – what is so huge?"

Lindsay walked away from him and fussed with folding a table runner made by her maternal grandmother. "I just need a little change, that's all."

Evan looked at her in disbelief. "Did you quit your job?"

"Not yet. I'll talk with Mrs. Sinnott tomorrow. If she needs me to stay for a week or two, I will. If she can get along without me, I'll leave soon."

Evan shook his head and then unzipped his jacket and sat down. "You need to explain this to me – I don't get it. This makes no sense. You love this town as much as I do. What's going on, Lindsay?"

Lindsay ignored the question. She didn't want to lie to him, but she also couldn't tell him the truth. It was hurting too much to be so near and yet so far from him, and the baby was not going to be his reason for being with her. His reason for being with her had to be for love.

"Lindsay," he said sternly, "please explain this to me. You're not telling me what's going on. Have you tired of the quiet winters here? Is that it – you're going back to Boston? Come on, give me some idea of what's happening. Does Meg know?"

Lindsay took a sip of her tea to moisten her dry mouth. "I haven't told anyone yet."

"You haven't even told Meg? Do you know how this is going to break her heart? She was just telling me a few nights ago that you are like a daughter to her – she is completely crazy about you. I don't get this. Could I have some tea?"

Lindsay was startled by the question after him ranting about what she could or could not do. "Yes, there's a pot of tea next to the stove – the mugs are on the shelf."

Evan stood and walked to the tiny kitchen, poured himself the hot brew, and returned to stand by the hearth.

Lindsay tucked the table runner and a small figure of a bird in among the clothing and other soft items, then she folded the top of the carton over, almost as if to conceal it.

She could feel Evan's eyes on her every move and finally she sat down and took a few sips from her tea. Evan sat down across from her and they were silent for a long while.

"Is it because I didn't tell you right away about Keith being well again? I thought you'd forgiven that of me – we had a nice dinner with him and little Sean. I told you all about Mary Ann. Is that what this is, Lindsay? Are you mad at me? Because if that's what this is, please, please don't do this. There is so much for you here. You have friends, a good job, and there's Meg."

Lindsay listened – he had not said a word about himself being in her life.

Lindsay stood, walked to the kitchen, refilled her cup, and then went back to sit down. Evan watched as he waited for some response.

"I need to work a few things out," she said. "I moved here for many reasons and I expect to be back – maybe in a year or so."

"A year?" Evan asked incredulously. "Lindsay, what is going on?"

When she didn't answer him he shook his head, placed his tea down and slipped his arms into his jacket. Without any further words, he looked at her, looked around the cottage, then left.

As the door closed, Lindsay stared at its solid form and then she cried. The remainder of the day she spent walking in circles – what would she take, what would she leave, and where was she going? She thought about Boston – she could not endure that familiarity at this time. Neither did she want to return to her aunt's and uncle's home – they would ask too many questions and she was not prepared to explain that she'd fallen in love with someone emotionally unavailable. Furthermore, due to a lull in her good common sense, she was now carrying this man's child.

In the early evening, the telephone rang and Lindsay let it go to voice mail. When she heard Meg's saddened and anxious voice, she picked up the phone.

"Lindsay, please don't tell me this is true. Evan said you're leaving Cliff Point."

Lindsay took a deep breath. "Yes. I was going to tell you tomorrow after work, after I had spoken with Mrs. Sinnott."

"But why?" Meg gasped. "What's happened? We're devastated."

Lindsay wondered who else besides Meg was devastated by the news, but she didn't ask.

"I'll come back at some point," Lindsay said. "It's just a time filled with complications – I need to get away for a while."

"A while? Evan said a year. Lindsay, that's a lifetime."

"I wish he hadn't told you," Lindsay said. "I wanted to explain everything tomorrow when I'd had time to think."

"Please don't be angry with him for telling me. He arrived here this afternoon and he just left – he's distraught. Lindsay, that man is crazy about you. Why do you think he didn't tell you right away about Keith being well enough to take care of Sean? He was afraid he'd lose you – he was trying to give it more time so that he could convince you to stay. I've never seen him like this."

Why, Lindsay wondered, had he not declared his feelings for her? Why did she need to hear them from someone else?

"I'm sorry," Lindsay said. "Evan has been a challenge. He recruited me for a very definite purpose. We accomplished what we needed to do, and he's never indicated that he had any real interest in me."

"But he does," Meg insisted.

"It isn't evident, Meg. He runs hot and cold. If anything, he's been evasive. I hardly see him since I moved back to my own place. It's hard for me to believe he cares if I stay or if I go. I need to make a change – just for a while."

Lindsay could hear Meg sigh. "I don't understand. Where are you going? I didn't think you'd ever return to Boston."

"No, I won't go back there to live. I don't know where I'm going – maybe toward the south for the winter. I have a friend from college who lives in Savannah. She's invited me to visit many times – I don't know."

"You're telling Lorna Sinnott tomorrow about leaving?"

"Yes."

"And when will you go?"

"As soon as it's convenient for Mrs. Sinnott. I don't want to leave her in a difficult position but before I went to work at the base she managed. I'll work it out with her. I could be here for another couple of weeks, or not."

"Whatever you do," Meg began, "please come and have some time with me before you go." Her voice was quivering – Lindsay felt sad that she was causing her very dear friend so much pain.

"Meg, I would never leave without seeing you first. We'll have a nice evening together – I promise."

When confronted with the news that Lindsay was resigning her position, Lorna Sinnott looked surprised. They had worked together as a team – the library had never been in such good form.

"If you could give me a week," the older woman said, "I think I could manage until we hire someone else. Honestly, Lindsay, you're going to be a hard act to follow. I've had every confidence in your work and rearrangement of the library – I'm not sure I want to hire someone in your place. If you decide to come back, please let me know. I would have you by my side in a heartbeat."

Lindsay smiled and hugged the rigid little body of Lorna Sinnott. "Thank you," she said. "I've loved working side by side with you. In the meanwhile, we'll have another week together."

It was decided by Lindsay that she would leave in eight days, the last Saturday of January. At four months of pregnancy, it was, in spite of sadness and reluctance, time to go.

On the Wednesday evening before she would leave, Lindsay arranged to dine with Meg. She had thought to invite Meg to the cottage, but with so many items put away or packed, they opted for dinner at Meg's.

"I can't believe this is our last evening together," Meg said with a shaky voice. "I can't tell you how overjoyed I was when you decided to come here to pick up the pieces and start a brand new life. This development, your departure for parts unknown, is absolutely stealing my strength. I can't believe it and I certainly can't understand it. But, I am not going to hound you about it anymore this evening. I just want to look at you and to talk with you – I want to extract as much happiness from this night as I possibly can."

"I want that too," Lindsay said. Near to tears, she took Meg's hands in hers. "You are family to me. I'll come back sometime, I promise. I love everything about this place."

"Does that include your husband?"

Lindsay sat back in her chair and said nothing.

"I'm sorry," Meg said. "I had no right to ask that question."

By Friday evening, Lindsay had said her goodbyes to her friends and had packed everything she intended for her journey. She decided to take a chance at seeing Sara, Ben, Adele, and Charlie. If Evan's car was there, she would go on – if it was gone, she would stop in. Driving close to his house, she could see that only Ben's car was there and she stopped.

Surprised to find the key still in her purse, she unlocked the front door and walked straight through to the wonderful old kitchen. There she was joyfully greeted by Adele and Charlie. She laughed and scooped them up in her arms, telling them how much she loved them. As she stood with the bundle of cats close to her body, Sara walked in to the kitchen with a smile on her face.

"I was hoping you'd come to see us before you leave," she said. "I can't believe you're going, Lindsay. We're going to miss you terribly."

Lindsay put the cats back down on the floor and went to Sara to deliver a hug. "I'll miss you too. I'm sorry that I need to go. I'll keep in touch though, and I'll be back at some point. I can't leave Cliff Point forever."

"I don't understand it," Sara said as she poured two cups of coffee and invited Lindsay to sit down. "I thought you and Evan had managed to find one another. Oh, I know how it all began. It was rough having to uproot yourself and move in here, but I had the feeling that after a while, you loved this old place the way that we do."

Lindsay choked back the tears and took a sip of black coffee. "You make the best coffee," she said to Sara. "And yes, I do love this house. But it's Evan's house – not mine."

"But it could be yours," Sara said.

Lindsay looked into Sara's beautiful hazel eyes. "I don't think so," she said.

"Oh, Lindsay, yes. If you were willing, yes."

"Why do you think that, Sara? This is a wonderful place – I loved every moment of living here. This kitchen is a culinary dream. The cats are adorable. You and Ben are like having a set of sweet parents – it's all amazing. But this is Evan's home, not mine."

"But I'm telling you, Dear, it could all be yours."

Lindsay wasn't sure what to say. She drank more of the coffee and asked about Ben.

"He's gone to the grain store. We were all out of bird seed; he'll be back soon."

"If it's okay, I'll stay for a while longer – I'd like to say goodbye to him too."

"He will be so glad to see you. He had hopes that you and Evan would be jetting off for a real honeymoon soon."

Lindsay swallowed a sip of coffee and looked at Sara. "Why would Ben think of that?"

"Because of the tickets and all the other plans Evan made."

"What plans, Sara?"

Sara placed her hand over her mouth. "Did he not give you the tickets?"

Lindsay looked puzzled.

"Come with me," Sara said as she stood and led Lindsay down the hall and in through the living room to Evan's work space. On a small desk where he kept his notes, there was a large envelope with the image of an airplane on its front.

"This," Sara said handing the envelope to Lindsay. "He was going to give you this. He was thrilled to be planning a future with you. I don't understand what happened."

Lindsay lifted the flap on the envelope and found two round trip tickets to Bermuda and a note.

My Darling Lindsay, please accept these tickets for a real honeymoon, and a wonderful life here with me. I love you beyond words. Evan.

P.S. I will not be sleeping on the sofa this time.

Lindsay read the note over and over, her eyes filled with blurring tears. She looked at Sara and then hugged her.

"Where is he, Sara?"

"I don't know. As a boy, he always went down to the wharf and watched the boats and the gulls when he was troubled. He might be there."

Lindsay took the note and left the house. The drive to the wharf was no more than five minutes but it felt like an hour. She parked her car and walked to the piers and then she saw him, his back to her, leaning against some rails. She stood for a moment, then walked within a few feet of him.

"Evan," she said.

He turned around slowly and when she saw his face, she knew – he was as in love with her as she was with him. She walked directly into his arms and they embraced so tightly that she wasn't sure where either of them began.

"Do you still mean this?" she asked holding the note and backing away just enough so that he could see what she had in her grasp.

"Absolutely," he half whispered and then his lips were on hers.

When they stopped in to tell Meg that everything had changed, she was overjoyed and asked Lindsay when they had a moment alone,

"What happened? Evan is glowing with happiness."

Lindsay leaned close to Meg and whispered, "I told him that I am four months pregnant with our baby."

Meg's hands flew to her face. "Lindsay Drury, you weren't telling me everything!"

Lindsay smiled.

"Boy or girl?" Meg asked.

"We'll find out next week if we have a little Caroline Amanda or a little Douglas William."

Evan came up behind her and wrapped his long arms around her. "Whatever we have, we're going to be the best parents anywhere, and we've made an agreement, more than one. As only children, we've been there – we want a bunch."

"Did I say a bunch?" Lindsay asked as she leaned back against him.

Yes," he said, "I believe you did."

Lindsay's Almond Angel Stars
(cookies)

1 cup soft butter (2 sticks of butter microwaved
for about ten seconds works)
½ cup granulated sugar
½ cup confectioners sugar
1 egg
½ teaspoon vanilla
1 teaspoon almond extract
2 ¼ cups of flour
½ teaspoon cream of tarter
½ teaspoon baking soda
1 cup of finely ground almonds

Mix all dry ingredients together,
then add butter, flavoring, and egg.

Shape these cookies into 1" balls; flatten them down with a spoon onto
a non-stick or lightly greased cookie sheet.

OR

Roll the 1" balls in a little flour; cut out star shaped cookies.

The tops can be sprinkled with sugar before baking, or can be lightly
frosted after they are cooled.

Bake at 375 degrees for between 6 and 7 minutes.
Makes about 5 dozen.